CW00456432

Path

to

Portugal

≈≈≈≈≈

Dawn Smart

Path to Portugal

Cover designed by Sally Marts, SdM Design
Cover photograph by the author

Please visit my website at www.dawnsmartllc.weebly.com

Published and printed by Amazon Publishing

ISBN: 9798713774974

Table of Contents

To the Reader

I wanted to include the Portuguese language in this story and hoped to make it as accurate as I could. I know I didn't always get it right and extend my profound thanks to Wendy Hagen Bauer and Andrea Wiley for their help in correcting my mistakes. My apologies for any missteps and for any mischaracterizations of the places I described in Portugal.

Chapter 1: *Escaping*

It wasn't a dreadful life, or a grim life, just a nothing life. Nothing exceptional. Nothing particularly interesting. Like the washed-out face staring at her from the hotel's bathroom mirror. Lank, drab hair held back with a plain barrette. Pale gray eyes. Sallow complexion. Maybe nice full lips but pulled down at the corners into an almost-frown. The face set atop slouched shoulders and a sunken chest. A picture of dejection. Gloom.

She had thought coming to Portugal on vacation, the first she had taken in more than five years, would be cause for celebration. It hadn't turned out that way. She had picked the destination at random from among many pamphlets at the travel agency. The bus tour, so carefree and fun-filled sounding in its flashy brochure description, was a relentless slog from cathedral to castle to beach and on to a ubiquitous shopping street. As much time had been spent sitting on lumpy bus seats and staring out smudged windows as exploring the sights. The hotels were second-rate, the restaurants not even that. And her tour mates? They were as dull and flat as she likely appeared to them. The boring nothing of a life she had sought to escape had followed her across the ocean.

Adrienne Martin rode the small stuffy elevator to the nondescript entryway, put her suitcase among the others of the tour group, and walked to the dining room, pondering with each step how she got here. *How had things turned out so disappointingly? Why is my life so meaningless?*

She looked back with deep regret. Passing up the chance to finish her university studies in literature, she had married a solid, kindly-seeming man, who turned out to be anything but. Uninspired in his work, he never went far in the company and was never truly happy there, transforming a decent guy into, at turns, a cranky complainer or a taciturn recluse. She had encouraged him to find something else, something more suited to his interests, but he wouldn't or couldn't make the change. And she, good wife she had tried to be and averse to conflict, stuck with him. Stuck. For thirty years. Thirty years in a bland New Jersey suburb. In a loveless marriage with occasional, unimaginative sex but without the delight and solace of children. Thirty years of piecemeal copywriting work on newspaper ads, brochures, catalog descriptions, and sales letters for local businesses. Thirty years of the persistent grinding down of her soul.

She might have protested or challenged her circumstances—did, in fact—but not strenuously and without the passion that might have carried her feelings into action. Cautioned by a critical and unsympathetic mother and without strong friendships where she could test more courageous scenarios, she repressed any thoughts about the need for change and simply stayed. Occasionally, Adrienne had toyed with the idea of leaving but had vacillated, unsure of herself. Unsure she could make it on her own. Always coming down on the side of *no, probably not, better stay*. And then it was over. In the winter of 1998, Arthur Martin died. At age 55. Leaving her an aging house in a working-class neighborhood and a small life insurance payout to supplement his retirement fund earnings.

So here she was, sitting alone at a table eating a mediocre breakfast at a crumbling hotel in Portugal. She gazed out the window at the local bus idling across the way, a piece of dry toast raised halfway to her mouth. She set it carefully back on the plate, stood, and went to the reception desk. Leaving a hastily scrawled note for the tour guide, Adrienne picked up her suitcase, walked out the door and across the street, boarded the bus, and took a seat in the back.

The highway twisted inland onto a narrower road leading toward the hills, back out to fog-bound beaches and the main highway skirting Portugal's northern coast, then east and through the green rolling countryside again. Three hours into this in-and-out, back-and-forth ride, on a sharp turn offering an expansive view, Adrienne saw a small town nestled in the steeper slopes. Although near enough and high enough to see a distant Atlantic, it was sufficiently far from the tourist-beckoning beaches to have escaped the development craze so prevalent along the shoreline.

Empty streets were lined with grey and white stone buildings, a few with wrought-iron balconies on the second floor. There were several shops with open doors to welcome customers, but a few storefronts with shuttered windows. The bus stopped on the small central plaza. A nearby café with a covered terrace seemed suspended over empty space—a sheer drop-off giving way to the flat expanse stretching to the far-off ocean.

Without much thought, Adrienne paid her fare, stepped off into the plaza, and walked to the café. It was not until she had finished the best meal she had had on her trip, *sardinhas assadas,* salty charcoal-grilled sardines, that she began to consider her situation. Finishing her coffee and a rich, chocolaty rice pudding, she paid the bill as she scanned the waning light of afternoon. A sudden chill made her reach for her Portuguese phrasebook. She beckoned the young waitress over and asked about a hotel, only to be told there were none. Another bus to take her on to a larger town up the coast? No, not until the next day. The waitress turned back to the kitchen as Adrienne made her way outside and sank onto a bench in the plaza. She pulled out the map, trace the route with a shaking finger, trying to judge how far she would have to walk. Too far. Slumped against a low wall, she mulled over her options. Although she had seen few cars on the small inland road, could she hitchhike? Slip into a side street and look for a secluded place to hole up for the night? She discarded both thoughts as too dangerous and just not things she could imagine herself doing.

Her heart hammering in her chest, her characteristic timid nature came roaring to life. *What had she done? What was she thinking?*

Out of the corner of her eye, Adrienne saw the waitress and a portly man with a dangling black mustache standing in the café door talking quietly. He wagged his head side-to-side and approached her.

In halting but clear English, he asked, "You are looking for a room? A place to stay?"

She sat up straighter and nodded, trying not to let him see her obvious relief.

"There is a place. Maybe not so good. But a place. Safe."

He introduced himself as Nicholau Neves, took her suitcase, turned, and gestured she should follow. She hesitated no more than a second. Did she have a choice? But the voices in her head were so loud she was sure he could hear them—*How stupid could you be? You're an idiot! How did you get yourself into this? Who knows where he is taking you!* It was her mother's voice as well as her own.

Three streets from the café he turned at a small alley, stopped at a door and knocked, pointing to a long row of grimy windows on the second floor. The door opened and a grizzled face peered out, scowling and muttering in a Portuguese much harsher than she had heard in her travels. The contentious exchange between the two men had enough headshaking for Adrienne to guess things were not going her way, but as she reached for her suitcase the gruff man stayed her hand, crossed his arms over his chest, and looked steadily in her eyes as if assessing the risk he was taking.

"OK," he said, followed by a string of comments aimed at her companion. The café owner translated in a hushed tone after her apparently new proprietor abruptly disappeared. Nicholau whispered that he was Lourenço Madeira, a local carpenter, and not really a bad person, just irritable sometimes.

Lourenço returned with a ring of keys, unlocked an adjacent door, and led them up a dark flight of stairs. At the top, two doors. He opened the one on the left, motioning them into a narrow room fronted by the windows she had seen from the street. Sparsely furnished with a flat couch against the back wall, an overstuffed chair with a torn seat cushion and protruding springs, and a floor lamp. A bank of cupboards and a small refrigerator sat below a long, cracked vinyl countertop along the windows. Lourenço gestured to the rear and mumbled *banho* before dropping the keys on the counter and turning back to the door.

"Wait! *Espere!*" cried Adrienne. "The cost for the night? *Custo? Preço?*"

He gestured vaguely and said, "*Vinte.* Twenty. OK?"

She nodded and reached into her bag, but Lourenço waved his hand with a curt, *amanha* and left her standing with Nicholau, embarrassed by the brusque behavior as well as the state of the room, musty-smelling and cobwebbed, clearly unused for some time. Adrienne brushed away his apology and used her limited Portuguese and most ardent gestures to thank him for his kindness and for finding her a place to spend the night.

She sat a moment on the edge of the single stool at the counter, then to give herself something to do, to fend off the creeping angst, she explored. At the end of the counter a cutting board flipped up to reveal a small sink and the cupboards held a hot plate, a collection of odd pots and pans, mismatched dishes and glasses, and a few pieces of silverware. The small closet by the entry turned up a reasonable-looking blanket and pillow and a dingy set of towels. She turned on the lamp, only to find a burned-out bulb, so switched on the bathroom light where she saw old, chipped fixtures, thankfully, not too grubby. After a quick wash, she settled herself on the couch, burrowed into the blanket, and fell immediately asleep.

Chapter 2: *Beginning*

Adrienne had been in Veredas almost three weeks. Somehow, one day had rolled into the next. She had not actively made a decision to stay—it just seemed to happen, each day unfolding quietly. She got up, made herself coffee, sat at the window for a breakfast of fruit and fresh bread from the local bakery, then walked the three blocks into the main part of town. The bright petaled flowers in pots by many of the entryways drew her in. Further on, the soft green of the footpaths into the hills lessened her worries. The far-off ordered terraces calming her. The scents of heather, lavender, and thyme familiar.

A large lunch at the café late each day provided her main meal, as well as the chance to get to know Nicholau and the pretty young waitress Marissa. Nicholau insisted she practice a little Portuguese, which allowed her to hear about the goings-on in the village and learn about the locals.

At the end of the first week, she was overtaken by a cleaning frenzy. She wore herself out scrubbing the bathroom, countertop and walls, waxing the wooden floor, and washing the windows, at least the inside and what she could reach on the outside where they opened. The attack continued down the stairs to the stone steps. Coming out of his carpentry shop, Lourenço had watched her work on the entry with a sour expression but said not a word. He had accepted Adrienne's extended visit without noticeable surprise and with the help of her dictionary, negotiated a weekly rate they both felt fair.

The flurry of activity held at bay the nagging fear she was losing her mind. Each night, now plagued with insomnia, she tossed and turned and argued with herself. *What was she doing here? What did she think was going to happen? She should go home.* Somehow, she could not face the idea and rose each morning with a resolve to stay another day. To make a comforting nest for herself in this quiet place.

There was a bus trip north to the larger town of Aveiro to purchase bed linens, a new set of towels, and a small toaster oven. As she stepped from the bus on her return, Nicholau rushed out, gallantly relieving her of her packages and talking excitedly in both English and Portuguese about her stay in Veredas. Adrienne gleaned from his stream of conversation that folks were talking—everyone wondering about her decision, her plans. She could only shrug and say, "*Não sei.* I don't know."

On an afternoon stroll past a shop off the main street, Adrienne was drawn in by the old vase in the window shaped like a rooster. It was more graceful, less garish than those she had seen in the tourist shops during her vacation tour. *Fonseca's,* she discovered, was more expansive than the simple entrance and window display suggested. A mishmash of pottery and glassware, light fixtures, rugs, and castoff furniture. As she wandered the aisles, weaving through glass-fronted cabinets and chests with open drawers filled with lace and linens, she came upon the shopkeeper and greeted the tall woman with a soft "*Olá.*"

Between her dictionary and Doroteia Fonseca's rudimentary English, Adrienne learned of the *Barcelos* and the rooster's legend and meaning—love of life—a fitting present for herself, she decided. An hour later she left with an invitation to dinner later in the week and the vase and a small lamp, trailed by Doroteia's two sons carrying a red upholstered chair with an end table balanced on the seat. As they wrestled it through the entry door, Lourenço came out to observe, helped manage the trip up the stairs, and directed the boys to remove the tattered overstuffed chair—sending it back to their mother, if she would accept it, and to the garbage dump if not. As he looked to the second-story windows the next afternoon, he spied the vase filled with lavender and sunflowers. He couldn't suppress a smile.

≈≈≈≈≈≈≈

Adrienne peered into the cracked and pitted mirror, surprised by the almost ghostly face staring back at her. Despite the dim bathroom light, she saw a face more animated than she remembered. Slimmer, too, due no doubt to the weeks of modest eating and daily walks. Her hair was streaked blonder from the sun but messily pulled behind her ears to keep it out of her eyes. She remembered the beauty salon called Bella's on a nearby side street and made her way there after breakfast.

The small bell above the door tinkled as she entered. A youngish woman smiled at her from across the room, "*Um momento, por favor.*" She turned back to her client, spoke a few words, and walked over with a flow of Portuguese Adrienne could not begin to follow. *"Eu não entendo,* I don't understand," she enunciated carefully. "English?"

"No... uh... *um pouco...*"

"Please, let me help," came a voice from the slight woman with gray-streaked hair sitting in the styling chair. "I speak some English."

"Oh, thank you. I desperately need a haircut and I'm not sure my phrasebook and sign language are up to the task."

Adrienne sat in the adjacent chair and after introductions, a description of the desired outcome was transmitted to the shop owner. Her translator Leonor Couto, she learned, had been a schoolteacher. Retired now, and widowed, she grew flowers and herbs for the local market and café.

Leaving the shop, Adrienne had both a new look and a Portuguese tutor. She would meet Leonor every other day for late morning coffee and spend an hour practicing. She found herself grinning as she made her way home, her previously limp hair now curling slightly and brushing the nape of her neck. She couldn't remember feeling so carefree, so hopeful, in years.

"Bom dia," she bobbed her head at Lourenço as she turned into her street. Then stopped. He was directing a young man on a tall ladder leaning against the building. The second-floor windows were being washed!

She smiled timidly. *"Obrigada."*

Lourenço grumbled something unrecognizable but nodded back.

≈≈≈≈≈≈≈

Time slipped away. Her days settling into a routine—coffee and breakfast, out for a walk somewhere or her lesson with Leonor, the late lunch at Pap'açorda, Nicholau's restaurant, and the occasional trip to Aveiro. Her growing language skill made it easier to fit into the life of Veredas. She could greet neighbors on the street, make her needs better known to the grocer, have more nuanced conversations with her friends, and gossip with Marissa.

The first dinner with Doroteia and her husband Rehor, a full head shorter than his stately wife, and their two sons and daughter turned into a regular affair. These were boisterous occasions, often including others from the village, where Doroteia proudly served old family favorites, mostly foods Adrienne had never tried—fava bean stew, clams, salt cod fritters, and sausages of all kinds. It was an adventure, in culture as well as cuisine. Rehor, whose English was quite good, told funny tales of tourists encountered on his bus-driving route. The children shared stories from school and plied her with questions about America. Adrienne answered in a mix of English and Portuguese, eliciting giggles and gentle corrections. She told the family a little about her life in New Jersey, her husband's death, and satisfied their curiosity about her non-decision decision to stay in Veredas with a shrug and small smile, "*Parecia uma boa ideia,* It seemed like a good idea."

And now, she had a cat. Coming home one evening it had twined around Adrienne's ankles while she fumbled with her keys. Dashing up the stairs ahead of her, the gray-striped tabby meowed at the top and waited patiently for the apartment door to be opened. She, well maybe a she, stalked around the room, leaped on the counter, and settled herself to look down toward the street. Gatinha became a regular visitor. Lingering on the stoop and mewing until she was let in, settling by the windows, and jumping onto Adrienne's bed in the morning to signal it was time to leave. Lourenço shook his head when he observed a morning exit.

Chapter 3: *Unfolding*

In the course of her Portuguese lessons, Adrienne was introduced to Leonor's spacious garden, partially hidden from the street next to the house. She admired the early-summer herbs and flowers and shared her own passion for gardening, describing the attempt to create a beautiful, magical place in the backyard of her home in New Jersey. Using the Latin names of flowers and shrubs she had learned as part of that effort, she found they could easily identify those commonly seen in Portugal so Leonor could envision how it looked.

The two of them also walked the paths above the house to see plants growing lush and wild in the hills. Lavender, rue, heather, thyme, thistle, mint, and rock roses. All abundant. One day returning from a walk she commented on the woven wreaths, the sweet-smelling sachets, and the handcrafted candles throughout Leonor's home.

"You know products made from lavender and other herbs are very popular in the U.S.," she told Leonor. "You could make a good business selling these to American tourists. All you have to do is add a pretty Made in Portugal label and you'd be set."

"Realmente?" Leonor looked over the top of her glasses to Adrienne. "Do you think they would buy something so simple?"

"Ai sim! They are all looking for something to bring home. The wreaths may not work so easily, but the sachets and candles would be easy to pack. And packages of herbs? Even

better. Something distinctively Portuguese, even if they are available back home."

They sat at the kitchen table and talked about the idea. What products she could include. How to package them. The name of a company. The more they talked the more enthusiastic Leonor became.

"I've been wishing for something more to do with my life. I retired early, to provide care for my mother, who is gone now. So, I help my daughter Valera and play with my grandchildren. Attend church. Tutor at the school. Grow the flowers for Nicholau and the market and make these things to give away as presents. I never thought of selling them."

"I'd be happy to help you. I know a little about enticing and effective messages." She had to use her dictionary to find the last words.

In the next few weeks, the concept for the endeavor grew. Leonor experimented with herbal and flower combinations and taught herself how to make a simple soap. She began to picture the product line. Adrienne created several label options for Leonor to consider and drafted a mock-up of a brochure, highlighting the hills around Veredas. On a trip to Aveiro they found a printshop to produce the labels and brochure and explored packaging materials, Leonor preferring a simple, rustic bag that could be used for all the creations, each with its own distinguishing label. She also talked about possible sales venues with her daughter Valera, who sold real estate in the region.

With the encouragement of Leonor and Doroteia, Adrienne had also begun to volunteer as an English tutor at the local school. Her Portuguese was by no means fluent, but it was better. Good enough for the task, said the principal, an older man she had met at one of Doroteia's dinners. He introduced her to the teachers who were enthusiastic about the idea, stilling some of Adrienne's anxiety about the prospect of a room full of apathetic kids. The teachers reassured her, noting how it would be a novel activity for them. So, once a week she sat with a group of students gently correcting their pronunciation as they read aloud and leading a conversation about their town, their lives, and current-day affairs they saw on television or read in the newspaper. There was a good deal of laughter in the classroom as they stumbled through the grammar and attempted to understand the Portuguese words Adrienne struggled with. But the students returned each week and even brought a parent.

It was through these sessions Adrienne became acquainted with more of Veredas's residents. The teacher who joined to help and to polish her own English-speaking skills. The baker's wife, who wanted to add a coffee shop to the bakery to draw tourists who hiked in the hills. Ileanna Neves, Nicholau's wife, who came because she wanted to know Adrienne better since she ate at the restaurant almost every day. When they learned of Leonor's new project, and Adrienne's part in it, the adults' discussion often turned to how the town could grow.

Adrienne was intrigued by the ideas she heard and wondered if she might be a part of it. Then, in those still sleepless nights, although there were fewer of them, she would chastise herself, plagued with doubts and questions. *What am I doing here? Why am I staying?*

Chapter 4: *Returning*

Adrienne could not put it off any longer. When she finally called to listen to the messages on her home phone, there were several from Connie, an acquaintance from the local crime watch group, about the neglected state of the yard. Adrienne heard her concern about the effect on the neighborhood and cringed, feeling guilty. She hadn't wanted to face the decision about returning home. Her mid-night conversations had not given her any answers. She admitted to herself, in the dark on her sleeping couch, that she didn't want to go back to New Jersey, but she was unsure what she should do. She allowed herself to dream, lulled herself to sleep with the idea that she would stay in Veredas. But increasingly, she woke to the light of morning with a demoralized sense of just how far-fetched that dream might be. *Aren't I just deluding myself? Ignoring reality?* To be so bold as to imagine a new life—it was so unlike her.

She had broached the subject with none of her new friends, feeling sure they would laugh at the idea of her staying in the village. As she frowned her way through a lunch at Nicholau's, he approached her table and asked whether there was a problem with the fish.

"*Não é bom*? No good?"

"*Não, não. É delicioso!*" she tried to reassure him. Then gestured for him to join her. "*Estou... incerta... confusa...* I don't know what to do," she finally cried out.

Nicholau listened intently as Adrienne explained, in English and Portuguese, her dilemma. He leaned back in his chair and said, "*É simples. Você fica.* It is simple. You stay."

He went on to share the story of his father's move to Veredas. It was unusual at that time, he said, for people to leave their ancestral homes, but there were four brothers and strife among them about running the farm and the winery.

"My father was the youngest, with no say in the decisions. He was frustrated and quarreled with his father and his brothers." Nicholau went on to describe his father's itinerant work, traveling from one town to the next and taking whatever job he could. How he had landed here and worked for the family who owned this restaurant. Doing whatever needed doing, filling in wherever he was needed, including the kitchen.

"After a time, when my father told them he was going to move on, the restaurant owners offered to bring him into the business." Their two sons had died in the First World War. There was no one to take it over, they had said. He fit in, he was a good cook, and they all got along. They needed him. It was his decision, of course, they said, then added, *Por favor, você fica.* And he did.

"My father told me when I came to work here that it was my choice, but he hoped I would stay, too, rather than move to the city where some of the other young men were going. *Por favor, você fica.*"

Adrienne saw the straightforward way Nicholau assessed her problem. No agonizing about whether it was fitting, what people would say, whether it made sense. It was just a decision. Did she dare?

≈≈≈≈≈≈≈

Adrienne buckled her seatbelt and settled back, her mind still bouncing between *It was fun while it lasted.* and *You can do it! You can change your life!* She felt no more ready to make her decision than she had been a few days earlier when she had made the plane reservation. She had put it off as long as she could, but the practical, good girl in her could not ignore the responsibility she felt... to what? Her dead husband? Her mother? Her neighbor? The image she held of herself?

She ordered wine—two small bottles—and sipped from the plastic glass and stared out the window at the white and gray clouds below. At nothingness. Like her insides. Empty but for the conflicting arguments in her head. As she drifted off, she told herself she would know the right answer when she woke. Just as she had told herself every night of the last month.

Touching down in Newark, Adrienne was drained and bleary-eyed. Untethered. She waited for her suitcase among the other passengers, seeing the same looks of exhaustion and disorientation. Hers grimmer than the others—tanned people returning home from vacations on some sunny beach. The shuttle to New Brunswick seemed interminable, stopping multiple times to disgorge tired travelers in places looking no different from her own suburban town. But the walk from the taxi in her driveway to the front door went far too quickly as she hurried past a forlorn-looking scraggly yard. The neighbor was right. The house looked abandoned. She could feel a cloud of despair hovering above her head. She almost looked up to see if it were visible.

Adrienne moved through the stale air of the house, opening windows and the door to the backyard. She stood on the small porch surveying the brown and drying grass and the wreck of her flowerbeds. The summer heat and humidity were dissipating, allowing her to breathe in and enjoy the familiar smell of the garden despite its sad state. She turned back inside to find her bed. Oddly, she slept well her first night back and when she woke ten hours later, it was with a sense of disbelief. *Am I really home?* With a shake of her head, it came to her immediately, *No. This is not home.*

Similar to her frenzy in Veredas, Adrienne's days filled with activity. First, calling a lawn and garden service to come and get the yard under control. Then, methodically cleaning each room of the house. Not just cleaning but sorting through a lifetime of accumulated belongings. She went from the living room to the bedrooms to the kitchen, emptying drawers and closets, removing worn drapes and throw rugs, boxing up books and now-meaningless collectibles. Discarding almost everything. At the end of each day, she drove a carload of unwanted possessions to the local thrift store.

By week's end, with only the garage and her garden shed left to tackle, she took a break and stopped by her neighbor

Connie's, to apologize for not answering the emails and for her sad-looking yard.

"I didn't expect to stay beyond my vacation in Portugal, but things just happened. It kind of grew on me. I'm not sure exactly why, but I love it there. I'm thinking about selling the house and going back."

"Really? How... um, how exciting." Connie did not look entirely convinced about the wisdom of the decision.

"I know, I know. I'm sure it sounds pretty odd. But without Arthur here, I don't have the same attachment to the house, the neighborhood. And for whatever reason, this town in Portugal, and some of the people there, have..." Adrienne's words drifted off. *Have what?* she asked herself. "Wormed their way into my heart, I guess," she finished, for lack of any better description of what she felt.

The exchange with Connie was simpler and less fraught than the one she would have with her mother. Irene Banks, at age 75, had bought a condo in a building north of Camden, near Adrienne's brother and his family. She and Andy had not been close. They had gotten together a few times a year for holidays and the occasional birthday. After their mother's move, however, they had talked more frequently about how things were going.

Sure, Irene might miss her, but Adrienne guessed not much. For years there had been semi-regular, but short visits. Their relationship had been a difficult one and her mother had always had complaints–about her, the apartment management, the news. It was always something. She was dreading the exchange to come.

The drive to Camden was not a long one. *Not long enough* Adrienne thought, to figure out the best way to explain she was leaving. Adrienne wasn't sure how her brother would react to the news of the contemplated move to Portugal. He probably wouldn't be able to imagine her making such a bold change. But she could predict what her mother would say. And it unfolded precisely so.

"You can't be serious! Leave your home? Go somewhere so… so strange."

"It doesn't feel strange to me. It's a small town with lots of friendly people."

"But what will you do there? How will you live."

"I don't actually know." The niggling doubts rose in Adrienne's mind. *What was she going to do? Could she live on what she had? Could she make money somehow?* After another half hour of similarly tense exchanges and the inevitable litany of complaints, she drove to her brother's house for dinner. She felt the gloom of her initial arrival descending again. Sure he would echo their mother's worries and skepticism, she did not relish the coming conversation. She drove even more slowly and sat in her car a while as she tried to regain some of her previous optimism about the idea of selling the house and moving.

But Andy surprised her. "Good for you," he said and laughed, pushing his longish hair from his forehead. "I can just imagine what Mom said. Not very encouraging, huh?"

"No. In fact, her questions raised some doubts... well, fears, I guess. I don't know how I'm going to live or whether I'll have enough money or if it's even a good idea or... " She ran out of words, spread her hands wide, and looked at Andy helplessly.

"Maybe you don't have to figure it all out now. You can go back there and try it out. If things don't pan out, come home. No shame in that."

"Well, Mom will certainly label it a failure. One she warned me about. I'd never hear the end of it."

"You know, I never said anything, but I often thought you listened to her, let her influence you too much. About Arthur, I mean."

"Arthur?"

"Yeah. He was such a stick-in-the-mud. Not at first, but later. Such a bitter, sour guy. But Mom always had an opinion and I know she told you to stay with him. She told me she had, anyway. Like it was somehow up to her to keep you on the right path. I thought about saying something but didn't. I'm sorry."

Adrienne was dumbfounded. Not about his characterization of their mother, or that she would have voiced her views on Adrienne's marriage, but that Andy had thought about it and toyed with the idea of intervening. It made her wish they had been closer, and she had known him better. He might have been an ally.

Her voice was soft, quavering, as she said, "We didn't see each other much. You and I. Didn't get to know each other as adults. I'm sorry for that." She leaned over to give him a tentative hug. He returned one more firmly.

The remainder of the evening Adrienne described Veredas and the people she had met. Andy caught her up on his job as a computer systems manager and his recent divorce.

"If I didn't actually like my job, I'd think about joining you in Portugal. It sounds wonderful. But I do like it. All kinds of things are opening up through the internet. It's an exciting time to be in the business."

"You can always come visit. It's a little place, but there's good hiking in the hills and it's not too far from the ocean and the beaches. I'd love it if you came."

"Well, count on a vacation visitor. Now that CiCi and I have split I can go where I want, not just to the shore like she always wanted. And don't worry about Mom. She'll make her peace with it in time, and if not, so what? I tune her out when she goes on and on."

"Now I feel kinda bad about leaving you here to deal with her," Adrienne said, sinking back in her chair. "Not that I did much except visit occasionally. You'll have it all on you now."

Her shamefaced expression resulted in vigorous headshaking from Andy. "It's not a big imposition. I see her once a week. I don't mind. And she likes it where she is, even if she complains about it."

"Still... " she bowed her head, so thankful for Andy's goodness. "You are a good man. A good son. A good brother." She reached over to put a hand on his shoulder, then up to tousle his hair. "And what's with this? I don't remember it being so long."

He chuckled a little sheepishly. "Another fallout from my split with CiCi, I suppose. Like... see, I can do whatever I want now."

Adrienne pondered the conversation with her brother on the drive home. She was encouraged by Andy's response and knew her mother would be fine, despite the grumbling that would no doubt continue. A little of her hard-fought-for confidence returned and she went to bed with a firmer conviction about her decision. The nighttime demons let her sleep.

Chapter 5: *Action*

With the magic of the lawn service and daily watering, the grass had greened up and the flowerbeds taken on a semblance of their earlier structure and beauty. Just a semblance—more than three months of neglect was hard to overcome. When the real estate agent arrived for a Saturday morning appointment, Adrienne started the tour in the backyard.

"From your description, and knowing you've been away for a while, I expected things to be in much worse shape. The yard is lovely. A nice combination of shade and sunshine for the flowers. Such a variety. You clearly worked hard to make it so." Beth was nodding and gesturing as she walked through the grass.

Adrienne preened a bit. The garden was, she felt, her one accomplishment. "Thank you. The garden was my sanctuary. Both doing the work and sitting there at the end of the day to relax and admire it. It's not what it could be right now, but if someone has an interest in it, they could bring it back to life."

"It's also so nicely screened in back from your neighbors. That's a great selling point for this area. As are the big trees in front."

"You should probably warn them, those big trees mean a huge amount of raking in the fall."

"We won't mention that. Let them figure it out on their own." Beth laughed and turned toward the house.

As they headed inside, Adrienne pointed out the renovations that had been made to bring the garden into the otherwise unexceptional house. The circular patio and brick grill off the porch. The large windows in the open style, up-to-date kitchen, and the adjoining den Adrienne had claimed as her office.

"The house is old. Nothing special. But we took care of it. Did necessary repairs. And tried to make this back part more comfortable and inviting with the connection to the yard. The street isn't busy, but the front of the house always felt a little exposed to me, so we didn't change much there and didn't use it much once we remodeled the back."

"This is a great space. I can see why you'd want to spend your time here."

The trip upstairs to see the two bedrooms and the bath was short. Ordinary rooms without much embellishment. Repainted and re-carpeted, but no major upgrades.

"The closet space isn't much to speak of. That's something people care about today. I guess we're all accumulating things and need the storage."

"The garage has some cabinets that worked okay for us. But it's not heated, so not a perfect solution."

"No, not something to feature, but we'll include it in the listing. Let's take a look."

As they made their way to the garage, Adrienne led the agent along a stone path, past the garden shed she had had built. "I haven't cleaned here, yet, so it's a bit of a mess. But it's a perfect place to work. And it's big enough to store everything a gardener needs."

"It might be something we can use as part of the sales pitch... A house for the gardener in you."

"As I said, it's been a sanctuary for me. I would love to think someone else will find it so. It's the one thing I hate to leave. Now," said Adrienne, "to the garage. Again, a mess, as I haven't gotten to it yet. I'm afraid it'll take me some time. There's a ton of stuff in here. Probably like all garages… the place we stick things we aren't ready to toss out."

They returned to the kitchen to talk through the details of the listing and pricing. Beth was optimistic about the sale and the price they might get. When she suggested an asking price, Adrienne's eyes widened.

"Really? I never dreamed it would be so much! It's more than I hoped for."

"It's an okay neighborhood, not far off a main highway, but the street is quiet. And the communities around here are changing. Gentrifying, I suppose. More people are considering them. The house is in good shape, and the remodeling in back and the garden make it special. I don't think you'll have any problem selling quickly. You said you hope to."

"Yes, I do. I didn't realize it until I came back, but I've grown attached to this small town in Portugal. I can't tell you how much I miss it and I've only been away for a couple of weeks! Completely unexpected. And so unlike me to be so impetuous!" Adrienne raised her chin, "But the idea of moving there has grown on me. I'm going to give it a try."

The following few days flew by in a whirlwind of busyness. Adrienne got up each morning, had her breakfast, and jumped in with her clean-up work. The garden shed was easy enough. Old pots, worn gloves, broken tools and half-empty bags of soil amendments and fertilizer she threw in the garbage; the better pots, tools and unopened bags of soil she took to a friend from her garden club and suggested they be given away at the next neighborhood sale. That left window washing and scrubbing the garden bench and storage shelves. The garage was another matter. She called Andy.

"You were so encouraging the other day. I can't tell you how much it lifted my spirits. I've decided to go ahead with my plan."

"Good for you! I am so excited to hear it!"

"Thanks. And…" she hesitated, not one to lean too much on other people, maybe especially family. "I've got a favor to ask. I had a real estate agent come out to get me started with selling the house. She was quite enthusiastic about it. Thinks I can get way more for it than I was imagining."

"Terrific! I know you put a lot of effort into the backyard and the remodeling. So, what can I do to help?"

"I've cleaned out the house and whipped the garden back into shape, but the garage is a huge mess. It's so full of stuff I can't park the car in it. I'm a little overwhelmed. I mean, I know I can do it, but I'd like to get it done as soon as I can so the house can go on the market."

"I'd be happy to help. I can come over Saturday. It shouldn't take more than a day, and if it does, I can sleep over."

"I think it will take longer than a day. But I'd love to have you stay. I'll spring for a good dinner out. It's the least I can do."

With that underway, Adrienne called the financial advisor she and Arthur had talked with on occasion and scheduled an appointment. She might as well face the facts about her fiscal future. She sat on the edge of her chair in his office, palms smoothing her skirt and trying to still a jiggling knee. Again, she was pleasantly surprised.

"The market took off at the beginning of the year. It's been doing nothing for the last few years and all of a sudden, things are happening. You've done well with the insurance money we invested, and Arthur's retirement fund is growing nicely."

She sank back, exhaled audibly, and felt herself tear up. The man reached into his desk and brought out a box of tissues. She took one, and a moment to compose herself, then told him about the plan to sell the house and move to Portugal. How she had feared she might not be able to afford it.

He looked at her closely and asked gently, "Are you sure? I mean… I don't know you all that well, but it seems like a pretty big step."

"I know. And really not like me," Adrienne took a breath and went on, "but I've thought a lot about it and decided to give it a try. I've spent the last few months in a small town over there and kind of fell in love with it."

"Have you thought about not selling, just renting out the house? That way you'd still have it if things don't work out."

"I did consider it. But I don't want to stay in the house. I feel like I need a fresh start. No matter where I end up."

He studied her another moment and said, "I admire your courage. I'd like to imagine I would be so bold."

"I've never thought of myself as courageous. Not even close. No one who knows me would say so either. And who knows, this may be a mistake, but I feel like I have to do something different. Otherwise..." Adrienne's voice trailed off and she looked at the hands twisting in her lap, back to the man's kindly face. "I'll feel like I've done nothing with my life."

It was quite an admission for Adrienne. One she had not permitted herself to voice out loud, but one that had been in her mind since her first nights in Veredas.

The look on his face was admiring, encouraging. He went back to the folder on the desk in front of him, "Financially you're in okay shape. Given the predictions about the market—although we can't bank on it—you should be fine. I can adjust a few things to make sure you have a safety net, keeping the retirement fund secure. And eventually, you will have Social

Security, too. You'll be able to take Arthur's first, holding off on your own until later, but not until you're sixty."

Adrienne released her shoulders, now aware of the tension she'd been holding. She hadn't realized how deeply apprehensive she had been. How fearful something was going to get in the way of her decision. The house. Her mother. The money. Her own anxiety. She left the office with a smile on her face, her step livelier, her heart lighter.

Chapter 6: *Closure*

Andy showed up early on Saturday morning, driving a flashy-looking truck, a thermos of coffee in hand.

"You have a truck! Since when?"

He grinned and said it had been a Christmas present to himself since he had not gotten a gift from CiCi and hadn't given her one either.

"That's a little mean."

"I deserve it," he threw back at her. "She got the house and the kids!"

"Sorry, sorry!" She hunched her shoulders and held up her hands.

"No, it's okay. I was being pissy. I hated the house anyway and the kids are probably better off. I still see them almost every week."

"I'm glad to hear that. They're good kids, and we both know having a father in their lives is important."

"Yeah, I hear ya. I do my best to be there for them. Hang out. Talk about stuff. Encourage them. Things you and I missed out on after Dad left. So, they're doing okay. Anyway… what's the plan here?"

"I doubt there will be anything I want. There might be things you do. I think we should pull everything out into the driveway and take a look. But I'm guessing it's off to the dump or the Goodwill for most of it."

When they opened the garage door, Andy whistled, "I see what you mean. Kind of a mess! Let me back the truck in and we can fill it up."

Adrienne began the sorting, pulling out broken lamps and chairs, outdated appliances, and half-done home projects. Lourenço came to mind. Maybe it was the woodworking tools she held in her hands. Arthur had been enthusiastic about building things for the house and the patio but abandoned them when they did not quite work out. He gave it up entirely as time went on. She realized Lourenço had been on the edge of her thoughts the last week. *What will he think of her moving back? Will he be pleased?* She shook her head to dispel the notion, sure he had not given her a thought and would be as surprised as anyone when she returned.

By noon they had made a dent, but the work yet to do was still daunting and the truck was full. After a lunch break and a trip to the donation site, they were back at it, hoping to get halfway through the task before dark. And succeeding with a second truckload, this time for the dump. A shower renewed their energies, and they shared an excellent steak dinner despite their fatigue and sore muscles. Sipping the wine, Adrienne probed for more about Andy's son and daughter.

"Kathryn is going to art school in the fall. She's pretty excited. She was accepted at Tyler School of Art, at Temple in Philadelphia."

"I remember her interest in art. I didn't realize it was so serious. Is she any good?"

"I don't know. She was sweatin' getting in, but she did, and got a scholarship to boot. So maybe she is. She'll have to live at home and commute, but with the scholarship it's manageable. I hope it works out. Not sure what she'll do with an art degree, but it's what she wants."

"How about Jake?

"Just one more year in high school. He's still sorting out who he is. Reads all the time—all kinds of different subjects. Loves history. Not sure where he got that! And he's good in sports, on the basketball team and does track. He's developed a new passion this summer—surfing! Drives over to the coast with friends almost every weekend. That might be the draw. A way to take off and be with his pals."

"Really! I had no idea New Jersey even had any surfing."

"I didn't either. But apparently, it's the best on the east coast, or so Jake tells me. It pushed him into getting a decent summer job, not the usual half-hearted lawn work he's done in the past. A real job at Campbell Soup that will pay for the car he wants. I'm just happy he got serious about something."

Adrienne propped her chin on her hands and leaned forward, "And how about you? How are you really doing?"

"I'm okay. Probably better than I've been for a while. CiCi and I argued a lot at the end. And now I don't have to feel guilty when I need to work late or when I want to spend a weekend fishing or off on my mountain bike. And like I said, I get to see the kids all I want. So being on my own isn't bad."

"I was going to say something, tell you you looked happy. Happier. And so fit! You've always been lean, but now... "

"It's the biking. I don't think I've ever been in such good shape."

Adrienne raised her glass in a toast.

Sunday was a repeat of their efforts, paying off with an empty garage, one more truckful for the dump, and another headed for Andy's with items he either wanted or was sure he could sell.

"It might take a while to get it to you, but I'll send you the money."

"No, no, no. You keep it. You've more than earned it. I can't thank you enough. This would have taken me all week. And it won't be much work to do a final cleaning. I can call the real estate agent tomorrow and get her started."

"Well, let me know how it goes. And we'll get together again soon."

"I promise. I'll be over to see Mom again. Maybe we can have dinner with Kathryn and Jake. I'd love to see them."

"They'd like it, too. I told them about your plans and they're dying to hear more about this place you're going to live. How you got up the nerve to move there. You're their hero."

That made Adrienne stand up straighter. She waggled her shoulders, "I've never been someone's hero before. I think I like it!"

He took off with a wave, and Adrienne went in for a well-deserved soak in the tub before dinner. She called Beth the following day and told her the shed and garage were clean and they could go ahead with the listing. The agent made a few suggestions about readying things for an open house and a tour for other real estate firms before that, a standard practice to give them wider exposure.

Beth showed up the next Thursday with a sign for the yard and shooed Adrienne out of the house.

"You don't want to be here when the agents drop by. They will be honest about things they don't like. It can be discouraging to listen to. You don't want to be here for the open house on Saturday either. It makes potential buyers anxious. So, now, off you go. Go shopping, to the movies, for a drive. Whatever. We'll be done by 4 o'clock. I'll call you tomorrow to let you know how things went with the agent tour."

≈≈≈≈≈≈≈

Adrienne drove off without the slightest idea of where to go, then thought how much she missed her daily walks in the hills above Veredas and drove the short distance to Rutgers Gardens. She could spend hours there enjoying the well-kept lawns and paths through the summer flowers. And Saturday she decided, she could visit her mother and try to arrange dinner with Andy and his kids.

Beth's predictions proved accurate. The house sold in six days. For the asking price. There were the usual back-and-forth negotiations, but the agent handled the details and a month later Adrienne was packing for the trip back to Portugal.

The final trip to see her mother proved more emotional than expected. Both were a little teary, an unusual circumstance.

"I can't believe you're going. I didn't think you'd really do it. I… I… I don't know when, or if I'll see you again."

"Don't worry, Mom. I'll come back to visit," Adrienne patted her mother's hand. "Or who knows, maybe you'll come see me!"

"Hah! That won't happen. I can't imagine." With this, she reverted to her more customary complaints and a discourse about foreigners and the cost of everything. Adrienne laughed, gave her a goodbye hug, and left for Camden for a more pleasurable exchange. Not only did she get to share a last dinner with Andy and his kids, but she had the fun of handing over the keys to her car to Jake.

≈≈≈≈≈≈≈

Adrienne sat back in her seat on TWA's flight to Lisbon, trying to calm the flutter of nervous excitement in her stomach. She felt sure she had made the right decision, reminding herself she could always return if things did not work out. But she wondered what people in Veredas would think. She hoped she would be greeted with enthusiastic smiles and "*Bem vinda de volta,* welcome back!" She closed her eyes and tried, unsuccessfully, to fall asleep.

Chapter 7: *Homecoming*

Exhaustion did not begin to describe how tired she felt, but as Adrienne gazed out the bus windows on the road to Veredas, she couldn't keep herself from grinning. The trip had been a long one, made longer by the transfers, from plane to shuttle, to train, and now this bus. But here she was, almost home. She had never seen it in fall. The harvest had turned green fields to fading gold and brown, but she relished the sight of the terraced fields and rocky outcrops now visible.

Taking the last turn up the steep street into the square, she felt a warmth spread through her. She wondered, *Would Lourenço still welcome her?* Adrienne looked to see if Nicholau's restaurant was open—not yet. It was midafternoon and Pap'açorda was closed until dinnertime, but she made her way to the side door, heard the rattle of cooking pans, and knocked softly, peeking into the kitchen. There was Nicholau, chopping vegetables and stirring a pot of stew on the stove, something smelling spicy and wonderful.

"Nicholau, *olá!*"

He turned and his round face transformed into a wide smile. Wiping his hands on his apron he crossed the room and enveloped her in a warm hug.

"Boa tarde! Bem-vinda de volta!" He stepped back and eyed her cautiously. "You are back? No?"

"Sim. De volta… home."

Turning to lower the flame on the stove, Nicholau removed his apron, picked up her two suitcases, and proceeded out the door, talking the entire time, faster than Adrienne's rusty Portuguese could follow. But it was clear, Lourenço still had a room for her. She trailed along, feeling a little shy.

"Você acha que ele ficará surpreso? You think he'll be surprised?"

Nicholau said no, that he thought Lourenço had missed her as he had been a regular at dinner, not typical of him. He then prattled on about the goings-on in town... What was new. What his wife and children were doing. Who was mad at whom.

He knocked on Lourenço's workshop door. Waited, knocked again. The whirr of a table saw quit and they heard steps approaching. His bulky frame appeared in the doorway and with a quick smile and a quiet *boa tarde*, Lourenço took her suitcases and led the way up the adjacent stairs. She gave Nicholau an amused look, thanked him, and said goodbye.

Entering her apartment, she was surprised to see improvements had been made—new green linoleum on the floor and a polished wooden countertop. She ran her hand over the fine-grained wood, feeling the silky smoothness of careful sanding.

"Lourenço! *É linda!* It's beautiful!"

He waved away her compliments and dropped the keys into her hand as he turned toward the door. She reached out to stop him, looking directly into his craggy face.

"Realmente, é linda. Such fine work. *Obrigada."*

He gave a bow of his head to acknowledge her thanks, closing the door behind him as he left. She stood in the silence. Fatigue overtook her. It was only five o'clock, but she was too tired to contemplate going back out for dinner. She unpacked a few necessities, quickly made the bed and fell into it; asleep within minutes. No demons plagued her dreams.

When she woke in the morning it felt as if she had never left. The familiar room, the sunshine, the quiet. She dressed and hurried out. She was hungry for both breakfast and a comforting routine. As she on the bench outside the bakery, sipping a steaming cup of strong coffee, Doroteia appeared.

"I heard you were back and was coming to get you for breakfast," she said, handing over a small bunch of flowers along with a hug. "For you, *bem-vinda de volta."*

After catching up on the news of her family and acquaintances in the village, Adrienne tried to explain her decision to return. How surprisingly easy it had been. And she told Doroteia about the improvements Lourenço had made.

"He asked my advice about the new flooring," she said. "What color it should be. When I asked if he would be renting out the apartment again, he just shrugged."

"Have you been to see it? Seen the countertop he installed? It is stunning!"

"I haven't but will drop in soon. I have to go, my sister is expecting me. And I imagine you will want to see Leonor.

She'll be so pleased you're back. She's started selling things with her daughter Valera's help, gotten her business going."

"I'm so excited for her. I'll head there now, with a stop to make an appointment at Bella's. My hair has been sadly neglected!"

"How about dinner to welcome you home? Tomorrow night? Who should we invite? Leonor. Maybe Nicholau and Ileanna, since it will be Monday and the restaurant will be closed. How about Lourenço?"

Adrienne gave her a slight frown, nodded and said, "You can invite him. He probably won't come. But..."

"What?"

"He seems different somehow. Not so... *mal-humorado*. Is that the word? Grumpy?"

Doroteia laughed. "Yes, we've all noticed. I even heard him whistling the other day!"

The dinner was an event with the five adults and Doroteia's and Rehor's children. Nicholau had them all laughing with tales of skipping school with Lourenço, once when they snuck off to see Carmen Miranda.

"She was visiting with friends at the Oliveiras. You know, the people who own the winery in the valley. We had seen her picture in magazines. The hats!" He threw his hands wildly around his head. "So funny! But Lourenço thought she was so glamorous."

Despite his clear embarrassment, Lourenço surprised them all by coming back with stories of their rowdier days growing up and one about Leonor and his wife, Jacolin. He went quiet at the end of that one and Leonor subtly moved the conversation to her new business.

"I've started here in the village—the grocers, Doroteia's, Bella's salon. And Valera gave some to a shopkeeper she knows in Aveiro and they have sold as well. I want to take things to a few more places she suggested. The sachets are easy to supply. They are simple to make. The herbs, too. The wreaths and soaps take more time, but I think they will sell, and for a good price."

There was excited talk around the table about other places she might try and other products.

"I haven't worked on the candles yet. They are more involved. I wanted to get myself launched before making them. And I'm not looking to start a big business, just a small one I can manage myself."

"You could hire us." This from Doroteia's oldest son Rehor, Jr. Rehe, as he was called. "We could work after school. Dinis and I." The younger brother nodded vigorously.

"Wait, wait, wait," cried his mother. "What about your schoolwork? Helping me in the shop?"

"We can do that, too."

"Por favor, por favor, por favor," chimed in Dinis.

Leonor laughed, "I'm not going to get involved in this discussion. But I'll think about what I might need if I want to make a bigger effort. I promise," she smiled at the boys and widened her eyes at Doroteia.

Adrienne re-established her walks and tutoring. Word of Leonor's small success with her business encouraged a few others to seek Adrienne's help with ideas to promote new enterprises. It was flattering, but she was not sure the skills she had were what they needed—creating marketing materials for a small home business was one thing, helping launch more involved efforts was quite another. Adrienne shared her concerns with Leonor.

"I'm not sure I should say yes," she frowned. "I would hate to have someone fail because of me."

"But you wouldn't be doing the work alone. Like with me. You gave me drafts to look at. I had opinions. I was the one who made the final decisions."

The more they talked, the more confident Adrienne became. *I could do this,* she thought. And it would be easier now. Andy had given her his old laptop computer. She had to figure out how to use it to create examples to show people, but he had assured her it wasn't that hard and the Computer 101 manual he'd included would help.

The conversation turned to Leonor's business and how far she wanted to take it.

"It's not just the work," she removed her glasses and rubbed her temples, "but the availability of the flowers and herbs. Remember, we talked about this. I have a large garden and it produces everything I have needed. More in the spring and summer months and I dry what I harvest and use it later. If I add more to what I am doing now, there won't be enough."

"I do remember. You thought you might find some other growers. Farms in the hills you could buy from. Have you thought more about it?"

"Yes. There are some of the people I might ask. Even Lourenço, but I haven't found the time to do it."

"Lourenço?" Adrienne's brow furrowed in confusion. "Does he have a farm? In addition to his cabinetry shop?"

"No, not a farm. But that house and big piece of property just up the road. We've walked past it many times. Admired the flowers, although the garden is overgrown."

Adrienne shook her head. "I had no idea it was his."

"He doesn't live there now. I think it was too hard for him after Jacolin died. And he had the apartment over the shop, so could move there. He's kept the house up but left the garden alone except for the most basic clean-up chores."

As she walked home, Adrienne thought about Lourenço and his house. The cheerless disposition he had exhibited when she had first met him. Clearly, sorrow had been at the heart of it and what kept him away from the house.

As she tried to sleep that night, she thought back on her feelings after Arthur's death and her lack of emotion when she had returned to New Jersey and sold the house. How little she had grieved. Both for her husband and for the house in which she had spent many years. It was obviously different for Lourenço.

Chapter 8: *Fall*

As fall deepened, Adrienne's walks with Leonor took on new purpose. They climbed different routes through the terraced hills, looking at the farms and the crops they grew. There were groves of olive and cork trees and long sinuous rows of wine grapes. Most fields were small, lying fallow with the stubble of cut grain. Leonor pointed out a few places with the pruned remnants of lavender, oregano, rosemary, and verbena shrubs.

"These are people I can ask. Most already have buyers, but they might be willing to sell me a small part of their crop."

"They might like the idea of selling to a local enterprise."

"Only if it doesn't mean less profit or require more work for them."

"You could hire Rehe and Dinis to collect it. Rehe is looking for any excuse to drive his father's car."

They talked about the approach to the growers and to Doroteia on the way back. As they passed Lourenço's property, Adrienne looked at the garden thoughtfully, wondering whether he would be included in Leonor's plan. She kept silent despite her curiosity.

It was late afternoon by the time Adrienne made it home. As she unlocked her door, Lourenço peeked out from the workshop and mumbled a string of Portuguese too fast for her to catch.

"Que?"

"I hoped you would join me for a glass of wine," Lourenço said in slower, well-enunciated English. "Tonight. On my veranda. It is still warm enough, I think." He nodded up the stairs to the apartment adjacent Adrienne's.

She didn't hesitate, "*Sim*. I would like that." She was curious. She had never seen his apartment.

When she knocked on the adjoining door that evening, Lourenço opened it immediately and ushered her through a short dark hallway into the light of a spacious room. There was a bank of windows similar to her own on one side and French doors along the front opening onto a roomy terrace. She had not been sure what to expect, but it was not what she now saw—books stacked on end tables and on the floor next to cozy-looking upholstered chairs, a richly colored rug covering much of the dark wooden floor. The walls were full of framed paintings. And to her surprise, a cat sitting at the entrance to the terrace.

"Gatinha, I wondered what happened to you!" She laughed and shook her head at Lourenço, "Cats are fickle. They take off when the spirit moves them. But I guess I did abandon her."

"She drops by on occasion. I think she likes to sit on the edge of the terrace and keep a lookout."

Adrienne made her way further into the room. More in keeping with her imaginings was a long table holding several in-process projects— a multi-drawered box with handles sitting ready to attach, a disassembled machine surrounded by its parts, a can of oil and a rag alongside a smooth, intricately-pieced cutting board.

Lourenço took in her curious look and her smile at his workspace, then gestured her out to the terrace and a comfortably padded settee. The table held a platter of *chouriço* and cheese.

"The cheese is Serra da Estrella and Cabra Transmontano, my favorites from the inland mountains. And this is the end of last season's sausage," Lourenço said, pointing to the *chouriço.* "Nicholau and I make it each year." He poured Adrienne a glass of deeply-colored red wine. "*Barco Velho*. It comes from the Douro Valley, near Porto where my daughter lives."

She sampled both the wine and the food, making appreciative noises as Lourenço explained the elaborate hog-killing, sausage-making, and smoking process, enjoying this glimpse of a man she realized she did not know at all. The conversation moved to other Portuguese food traditions, the woodworking projects on the table, and the wine from local vineyards. Adrienne complimented him on the one they were drinking and shared how much she enjoyed trying the different types in Portugal.

"I'm certainly no expert, but this is *deliciosa*."

The easy conversation continued as Lourenço asked about her tutoring and her work with people in town. This led to how well Leonor's business was going. She described the day's foray to the farms where they had seen the herbs and the plans to acquire more.

"Lourenço, your English is much better than I remember," Adrienne said. "Have you been holding out on me?"

"*Que?* Holding out?"

"Keeping it a secret."

"*Não.* My children took it in school. And now my grandchildren. I practice with them." He ducked his head and smiled, "And a little since you have returned."

She folded her hands in her lap, took a breath, and raised her eyes to his, "I wondered, if you don't mind my asking... Leonor pointed out your house. I didn't know it was yours. I wondered... why you live here and not there."

He took a large swallow of wine before answering. "My great-grandfather built the house, added to by my grandfather and father. I grew up there. My wife Jacolin died there." He looked out over the now dark street to the dimming sunset. "It was just too hard to stay. Everything reminded me of her. I had this place above the workshop and thought I would come for a little while. To get used to her being gone. But it has been five, no, almost six years."

He shrugged and Adrienne wanted to reach over and take his hand, but it felt too familiar, too intimate. She opted instead for a small smile and an "*Eu sinto muito*. I'm so sorry."

With a shake of his head, Lourenço said, "I have gotten used to it. It is easier to remember things she loved, things we shared. I put up some of her paintings. Come, it's growing cold, let's go in and I'll show you."

He straightened them as he led her around the room, pointing out the ones of his daughter, a few landscapes, and several of delicate flowers. "These were all done at the house. The garden was one of her favorite pastimes." He paused and went on, more to himself than to Adrienne, "Maybe it is time to think of moving back."

As she snuggled under her comforter that night, Adrienne thought of what she had learned about the man next door. A deeper emotionality and warmth than she had expected from the curmudgeon she first met.

≈≈≈≈≈≈≈

The days were filled with new work for Adrienne. The baker and his wife were completing their expansion of the café and she finished the draft of a flyer and a story they could send to the weekly regional newspaper. She made the changes they wanted, so happy she had taken Andy up on the offer of his computer. She took the floppy disc to the printer in Aveiro and when the grocer saw the flyer, he asked if she would help with the promotion of his new ice cream counter, slated to open in the spring. Although she was not charging anyone much, she was pleased to be bringing in the small amount of money she did.

Another event had the town talking—the head of the school was retiring, being replaced by a young man chosen specifically to help with the modernization of education occurring throughout Portugal. There was a gathering to honor the outgoing director and welcome the new one. When he was presented to the assembled group, he shared his vision of an expanded curricula and his hopes for a school that would become a resource for the whole community.

When she shook Senhor DeRosa's hand and introduced herself, Adrienne was surprised he recognized her name. "I have heard such good things about the English tutoring you do. I am hoping we can do more. Maybe, if you are willing, we could make it a formal part of our school day, not just an after-school group. Although I understand there are adults who are interested, too."

"I would like to tutor. I'm not a certified teacher... I don't know if it is required."

"We can look into it, but I don't think so. Tutoring is judged differently than teaching. We should talk further. I start officially after the first of the year, but my wife and I will move here next month." He shook her hand again and went on to greet another person.

Leonor, who was standing at her side, told Adrienne she had met Senhora DeRosa. "They're renting an apartment I own... well, it was my mother's before she passed on. It's only until they settle in and decide on a place of their own. She is very nice. Grew up in the mountain region east of here. Interested in the herbs and my new business. Who knows, maybe another helper. And..." she gave Adrienne a sidelong glance, "I saw Lourenço today. He was at the house, cutting back some of the overgrown plants. He offered me some of the clippings. Herbs to dry."

"Really, how wonderful… I mentioned our walk and visit to the farms to him the other night. Your hope to get some herbs from them."

Leonor gave her a sideways glance. "The other night? Oh, this is getting interesting."

"A glass of wine together. Nothing more." Adrienne nudged the smaller woman's shoulder. "But we had a good conversation. His English is better than he has led me to believe, so now when we talk it is in both Portuguese and English. It's easier. Anyway, I learned a little more about him and the house. And his wife. He showed me some of Jacolin's paintings."

Leonor shook her head, a small smile lighting her eyes.

Chapter 9: *A Move*

It was November, getting colder when Adrienne opened her mailbox to find a postcard from her brother.

> *Hey Sis, I was thinking I might come for a visit. Maybe for Christmas? Let me know if it's okay. Love, Andy*

She walked upstairs trying to puzzle out where Andy could stay. Her place was obviously too small, even for a cot or an extra mattress on the floor. Maybe Leonor's. Or better yet, Doroteia's sister. Benita was thinking about converting her house into a *pensão*. At dinner, she and Nicholau discussed different ideas.

"It would give Benita a chance to try out her plan," said Adrienne. "I know she's not ready to launch herself into the business of running a guesthouse, but she could see if she likes having people in her home."

"*Sim*, you could ask her. Who knows, she might like to try it. And if not, we can figure out something else."

The bell over the restaurant door chimed and Lourenço walked in. A not uncommon occurrence of late—him joining her for dinner or a glass of wine.

"What do you think, Lourenço?" asked Nicholau as he pulled out a chair. "Would Benita take in Adrienne's brother over Christmas? Try out her idea of opening a *pensão*?"

Lourenço cocked his head at Adrienne, "*Que*? Your brother is coming?"

Adrienne shared Andy's plan to come for a visit over Christmas and her need to find a place for him to stay. As he poured Lourenço a glass of wine, Nicholau listed the options they had talked about. Adrienne's—too small. The room over the bar on the other end of town—too noisy. Leonor's—not enough space with Valera and her family coming for the holiday.

"I would offer, but my son and his wife are coming, too. And Doroteia's got a full house. But maybe Benita."

Lourenço rested his elbows on the table, considering. "Benita might be willing. Wouldn't hurt to ask." He sipped his wine and asked Adrienne about her brother, what he did, what he was like. She gave a helpless wave of her hand as she explained how distant she and Andy had been but went on to share how much she had enjoyed their time together during her summer visit.

"It wasn't that we were indifferent or unfriendly. Just too busy with our own lives to spend much time together as adults. I guess it is not atypical for Americans. Many families don't see each other much, aren't as close as they are here in Portugal."

Both Lourenço and Nicholau shook their heads. "*Sim,* it would be unusual here. Even with my daughter and son-in-law living in Porto," said Lourenço, "we see each other every month." Nicholau nodded in agreement.

Lourenço was quiet on the walk back to the apartment and Adrienne did not press him for conversation. He said goodnight somewhat distractedly as she turned to her doorway and he to his.

A sharp rap on her door the next morning surprised Adrienne. It was early. Lourenço's puffy eyes and stooped shoulders concerned her as she waved him in.

"Are you alright? *Venha, sentar.* Come, sit." She pulled the stool to her windowed counter and took out a cup, offering him coffee.

"I am fine, thank you. *Obrigado.* A little sleepy. I was awake much of the night. Thinking. *Ficar em águas de bacalhau.*"

"*Ficar em águas de bacalhau*? Remain in codfish waters?" This was not a familiar phrase to Adrienne.

"*Sim,* it means an unsolved problem. I tried to sort it out last night, but I am unsure—unsure if this is the right solution." He hesitated, looking into his coffee. "Your brother is coming for Christmas. I am thinking you should move into my apartment and he would stay here."

"Move? Into your apartment?" Adrienne sat back and stared at him. "*Contigo?* With you?

"*Não, não, não!*" Lourenço put up his hands, palms facing her, and shook his head vigorously. "I am sorry. I wasn't clear. I will move to the house. To my house."

They sat in silence. Adrienne reached out and put a hand on his arm. "Are you sure this is what you want to do, Lourenço?"

He raked a hand through his hair. "*Não*, not really. But I think it may be time. And now I have another reason. A push—is that how you say it in English?"

"A nudge," Adrienne smiled. She finished the last of her coffee and said, "Maybe you should think about it a little more. It's a big step. You should not do it just because I need a place for Andy. And it's more than a month away. There's time."

She sent a postcard to Andy the next day, letting him know he was welcome anytime. She did not give any details about where he would stay.

≈≈≈≈≈≈≈

Three weeks later they were moving. Lourenço into his house and Adrienne into his apartment. He had emptied the closets, cupboards and drawers, leaving a decorative set of dishes, glasses, and a full complement of kitchenware. He took most of the books and all but two of Jacolin's paintings. With Rehe and Dinis's help, he also moved his well-used upholstered chairs and the living room rug, replacing them with similar pieces from his house. Over Adrienne's objections, he hired a cleaner who scoured the kitchen, bathroom, floors, windows, and terrace. As she walked through to consider what she would do to make the apartment her own, she could feel the echo of his life in the now-empty seeming rooms.

Her move was much easier—clothes, a few favorite dishes and kitchen utensils, and her books, the computer and files of the work she had been doing with people in town. She left everything else to ensure the smaller apartment was comfortable.

The to-do list to make the move complete was relatively short and the must-buy items easily obtained on a trip to Aveiro with Doroteia. A new warm quilt, pillows, sheets and towels, some colorful table linens. More was not needed. But as the two of them walked to the car after lunch, Adrienne spied another *Barcelos* rooster vase in a store window and knew she wanted it, allowing her to leave the original one in the old apartment. She also found a set of five framed drawings of wildflowers to fill the now blank walls of her new home.

While browsing she came across an oddly shaped wood and brass hand tool Doroteia said was used in the past in the cork trade. Adrienne had seen a collection of old tools displayed in one of the apartment's bookcases, not quite remembering if this shape was among those on the shelf.

"I think a housewarming present is in order, don't you?" she asked. "Is it reasonable? Can you ask?"

With a little dickering, Doroteia secured the items for Adrienne at a good price, plus a rather grimy pair of lamps. "I can clean these easily and they will go well with some nice lampshades I have at the store. My gift for your new home."

After a visit to Leonor the following day, Adrienne walked up the hill with her present and a lavender wreath. Lourenço swept open the front door with a flourish and a wide smile. "*Bem vindo a minha casa!* Welcome to my home."

Adrienne offered her gifts, saying Leonor had sent the wreath for his bedroom "to help him sleep with pleasant dreams". Lourenço unwrapped the hand tool and beamed. "It is not in my collection," and escorted her into a large living room with tall paned windows across the front and wide French doors leading to a stone terrace. The room was light and airy despite the dark paneling and floors. An ornately carved case held woodworking books and an assortment of tools. He moved a few to the side and place the corking tool on the center shelf.

"*Obrigado.* You should not have." Lourenço took her hand. "You have given me a big gift already."

Adrienne gave him a quizzical look. "*Que?*"

"Come, let me show you my house."

Lourenço walked her through a dining room that would have looked stately if not for the projects strewn across a grand polished table protected by newspapers, on into a library that looked out to a secluded part of the garden. It was clearly his favorite place as the cozy upholstered chairs were there surrounded by books. The stairs to the second floor were flanked by a sleek, curved banister he said had been crafted by his grandfather. After a quick peek into each of three bedrooms, they returned to the main floor, he noting with a chuckle a few chips in the newel post where he had ridden trays down the stairway as a boy.

Throughout the tour, they had made small talk and Lourenço had shown off the pieces of furniture or cabinetry made by his father and grandfather. On occasion, he had pointed out the needlework done by his mother or a painting of Jacolin's. And portraits of his grandparents, and his father and mother.

"Meu pai e minha mãe," he said, reaching out to rest a hand on the one of his father.

He led her through a remodeled kitchen with glass-fronted cabinets, broad countertops, and up-to-date appliances. Outside the back door was a screened porch looking over an overgrown kitchen garden and to the farms and fields stretching across the hillsides above the town. He pulled out a chair for her at the table, poured coffee, and set out a plate of cookies.

"Now that I am here, I realize how much I have missed this wonderful house. It is full of memories. Some sad, but mostly not. Even the garden—Jacolin's special place—also reminds me of my mother and grandmother and the things they planted. So, yes. *Eu sou grato.* I am grateful."

"*Não.* You would have come home, eventually. I may have speeded things up a bit, but no. I can see how you... " Adrienne thought a moment and said, "fit here. More at ease than I have ever seen you."

Lourenço leaned back and seemed lost in thought for a moment. "I don't think I admitted to myself that I wanted to come back. It seemed wrong, somehow. To come back and enjoy my life when Jacolin was gone."

"I know the feeling, a little." Adrienne stopped, looked down. "Although, it was different for me. My marriage to my husband Arthur was not happy like yours. We weren't as close as you and Jacolin obviously were. But after Arthur died and I came to Veredas, I was so glad to be here. Then I felt guilty. Like it was wrong to be so happy, knowing I never would have been, had he lived."

She stopped again and looked up at him and then away, her face reddening. "I'm sorry. I didn't mean to run on so. To talk about my marriage. You probably don't..."

Lourenço interrupted with a wave of his hand, trying to form his words carefully, using both English and Portuguese. "I wondered. I wouldn't have asked why you stayed when you first came here. But I saw how you changed. Became happier, more carefree. *Um espírito libertado...* a spirit set free. I could see it."

"It felt that way to me, too. Thus, the guilt. More so when I wrestled with the decision to sell the house in New Jersey. Could I come back here? Should I? Did I deserve this? A new life? Somehow, that spirit you talk about prevailed. And here I am." Adrienne relaxed her grip on her cup with some effort. "I don't know for how long. I don't let myself think too much about my future."

"It is hard for me to imagine you would give up the good feelings you have for your life in Veredas. Maybe it is... *lavar a égua,* as my grandfather would have said. Literally, it translates to wash the mare, but it means to do something you have long wanted to do."

They sat quietly for a time, then Adrienne smiled guiltily and said she had overstayed what was meant to be a short visit.

"But you will come back. Bring your brother when he is here. My daughter will be coming from Porto with the grandchildren. I would like you to meet them. Maybe I will have a party. To celebrate Christmas… and my return home."

Chapter 10: *The Visit*

The last days before Andy's arrival were a dizzying series of tasks to make preparations and finish work on projects she had undertaken. They had agreed he would take the train from Lisbon to Coimbra and Adrienne would arrange to pick him up there. It was more than a three-hour train trip, but it would give him time to get oriented and nap to relieve the jet lag.

Her old apartment was ready—cleaned, bed made, lavender and dried flowers in the *Barcelos* vase, the refrigerator stocked with snacks and drinks. She had made another circuit of her new apartment, moving things around and hanging the drawings she had purchased with Doroteia. As she went to bed, she thought through the meals she had planned, although there were several invitations from her friends in Veredas. And she hoped they would have the chance to tour a bit of the area. She had only been to a couple of nearby cities since her disappointing bus tour.

≈≈≈≈≈≈≈

Adrienne sat on the station bench, impatiently waiting. She was so excited to welcome Andy to her new home. Leonor had convinced her to borrow her car, a stick-shift such as Adrienne had not driven in years. She had left early, arrived early, and been waiting for almost an hour. The drive had been easy. She chided herself for her anxiety about driving in Portugal. There had not been much traffic on the roads, and she had mastered the unfamiliar car quickly.

Finally, finally, an announcement came over the speaker. *"Chegando de Lisboa, Track Dois."* She jumped up and looked down the track. There it was! Slowly, the train pulled alongside, brakes screeching. She scanned each window as it went by and then saw Andy, hair disheveled, hanging out of an already-open door near the rear.

"Hello! *Olá!*" he waved and stepped down as the train came to halt, dropping his suitcase and hugging her.

"You're here, you're here. I can't believe it!"

"The plane ride seemed like it would never end, but the rest of the trip has been terrific. Since my flight was a red-eye I thought I'd sleep but was too excited. Such beautiful country."

"Wait until you see Veredas. Higher in the hills. Rolling fields, mostly brown and dormant now, but vineyards and groves of olive and cork trees. Prettier, greener in the spring and summer than now, but the town is wonderful. Quaint, I guess. You'll see soon enough. It's not too long a drive. Do you need anything? Shall we get something to eat or drink?"

Andy laughed at her breathless chatter and grabbed his bag, "No, no. Let's go."

They caught up on news of their mother—who could not believe Andy was making a trip all the way to Europe to visit Adrienne—and his children—both doing well and thrilled their father was off on an adventure. And the rumor going around that CiCi had a boyfriend, a serious one.

"I may be off the hook for alimony soon! And the kids seem to like him okay, so that's a relief. They'll both be out of the house soon anyway."

It was mid-afternoon when they reached Veredas. Adrienne parked in the street and showed Andy up to the apartment, leaving him to get settled while she took the car back to Leonor. When she peeked in on her return, he was asleep. She backed out of the room quietly, leaving both doors between the apartments open. It was after seven o'clock when Andy surfaced.

"Sorry, I was going to lay down until you got back. I guess the jet lag kinda caught up with me."

"It's okay. I figured you'd need time to adjust. Are you hungry?"

"Famished!"

"I have things here I can put together. Or we can go out."

"Let's go out. It's late to start cooking."

Despite the beginning of a drizzle, they walked to Pap'açorda's where Nicholau greeted Andy with a big grin and a string of Portuguese, switching to his slow, precise English to welcome him.

"I didn't know if you would come tonight. I have *caldo verde*. That is potato and kale soup, with *chouriço,* our local sausage. Healthy for you, traveling so far."

He hurried off to the kitchen while Marissa set bread and olive tapenade to the table. She introduced herself in careful English, saying Adrienne had been helping her learn.

"Your English is quite good. *Boa!* See, I learned some Portuguese, too," Andy boasted.

Nicholau bustled back into the dining room bearing a bottle of wine. "This is one of my favorites, a good vintage *Bairrada* from a winery not far away. My treat for such a special occasion," he said, pouring glasses for each of them and raising his own in a toast.

"Felicidades e Bem-vindo a Portugal!"

With a rush of wind, the door opened. Lourenço quickly shut it behind him and approached the table. In a combination of Portuguese and English, he said, "I saw when Adrienne returned Leonor's car and knew you must have arrived. I stopped at the apartment to welcome you and no one answered, so I thought I would find you here."

Another chair was pulled to the table and a fourth glass of wine poured while Adrienne made introductions. Lourenço raised the glass and gave Nicholau an appreciative nod. "A fine year," he said.

Nicholau excused himself to see to the other table of patrons and the conversation proceeded with interruptions for translations and laughter as stories were told of Adrienne's first arrival in Veredas. Soon enough, the bottle of wine was finished, and Andy's eyes were beginning to droop.

"Come, let me drive you. It is raining now," said Lourenço. "Which is good. Rain tonight and tomorrow not."

≈≈≈≈≈≈≈

He was right. The morning brought sunshine and a walk through town with a first stop at the bakery for a second cup of coffee and a *pastel de nata,* Adrienne's favorite eggy custardy pastry. There were introductions to the baker and his wife who shared their pleasure at the success of the coffee shop, opened in late-fall, and their appreciation for Adrienne's help in growing the idea for it.

"Adrienne helped us think of ways we could advertise it," the baker said. "And how to make it part of the walking and hiking tours in the region," his wife added. "We have been less busy lately than in the warmer fall months, but even now we get tourists from Figueira da Fox and Porto almost every day." She reached over the counter to pat Adrienne on the shoulder. "*Obrigada,* we could not have done this without you."

They took a winding path through the streets of Veredas to Doroteia's store to say hello and promised to attend dinner the next night. On into the *praça,* where Adrienne showed him the church and the school where she tutored. She pointed out the plaque with so many names, telling him they were townspeople who had died during the war.

"Lourenço told me there was a story about this, but I haven't heard it and haven't had time yet to learn more about it."

They had been stopped more than a few times by town folk who knew of Andy's visit and wanted to welcome him, as well as tell him of their gratitude for Adrienne's assistance. Either with their English or with ideas for their businesses or both.

They continued to Leonor's for a quick stop to extend another thank you for the loan of the car. This turned into a tour of the business underway in her recently converted garage. Herbs hung from the ceiling rafters, wreaths in various stages of completion sat on a long countertop, and a young woman was stirring a sweet-smelling mixture over a large double boiler on a hotplate.

"This is Senhora DeRosa. Carolina, the new teacher's wife. She is helping me during the rush of Christmas."

The woman nodded her hello and apologized. "*Desculpa,* I am sorry. My hands are full, and this is at a critical stage. Almost ready."

They watched as she ladled the melted mix into a large measuring cup and poured it into individual metal forms arrayed down the length of the table alongside three rows of molds already filled. Carefully, she placed a small flower, a few petals or leaves on top of each one, shaking it carefully so a waxy film covered the decorations.

"There! And now it must set. Tomorrow we will wrap them and label them for delivery."

"I am so thankful Carolina joined me," said Leonor. "I would not have been able to manage the demand. Everyone told me they hoped to get wreaths and the soap for their Christmas sales."

"A *Feliz Natal* for everyone!" said Carolina with a sincere smile.

"And now, we'll let Carolina clean up while I set out a little lunch for us all," said Leonor. "I hoped you would come by and made something special."

Despite protestations it was unnecessary, Adrienne and Andy stayed to share the meal, helping set the table.

"This is *bacalhau a bras,*" Leonor explained. "Salted cod, onions, and potatoes cooked with eggs." She pulled the pan from the stove as Carolina joined them.

"Ummm," she said. "*Bacalhau a bras,* my favorite."

Over the meal, the conversation turned back to the business and the delivery of products to stores in neighboring towns. Carolina and her husband would be away, leaving shortly to visit her family for Christmas.

"My daughter Valera would usually help," Leonor said to Andy, "but she is ill with a cold."

"Maybe we could help," said Adrienne. "I was hoping to show Andy something of the area."

It was quickly decided that Adrienne and Andy would join Leonor at the end of the week to make the deliveries. They would make a day of it, with lunch in Figueira da Fox, a resort town to the south, a trip up the coast to view the seashore, and a meander along inland roads on their way back to Veredas.

Over dinner, smaller than planned due to the substantial lunch, Andy praised Adrienne for how thoroughly she had inserted herself into the town. And how people embraced and valued her.

"I can understand better now why you wanted to return," he said. "The town is great. And people clearly like you, want you to be a part of it."

"It's funny. When I returned here, everyone I know told me how glad they were to see me back. How happy they were I was moving here, not just visiting." Adrienne looked out to the terrace, lost in thought. "I lived in Brunswick for more than thirty years. I can't say anyone there misses me or even realizes I've left."

With a shake of her head, she changed the subject—the next day's adventure—a longer walk up into the hills, assuming the good weather held. Still feeling the effects of jetlag, Andy begged off another glass of wine and took himself off to the other apartment. Adrienne did a quick survey of her refrigerator and selected a container of olives and some fruit to contribute to Doroteia's dinner.

As she went to bed, she gave herself a little hug of happiness, and felt a bit of pride, in the pleasure of the day, their interactions with people in Veredas, and Andy's recognition of her place in the village.

Chapter 11: *Christmas*

Adventures filled the following days. A quick bus ride to Aveiro for shopping. Walks to take advantage of the winter sunshine. A fine lunch at Nicholau's to meet his son who had come for the holiday. Dinner with Doroteia and her family was its usual raucous affair. The typical fun was accentuated by the children's excitement about Christmas and the coming visit of their grandparents. Andy raved about the food, *pastéis de bacalhau,* fried fish cakes with onions and garlic. They left promising to take part in the baking of *biscoitos* that would precede the family's tradition of sharing the biscuit-like cookie in the town square on Christmas Eve.

At the end of the week, Leonor's delivery trip began with the loading of packages and a drive south to Coimbra, their first stop. The route took them further to Figueira da Foz where they dropped off more goods before lunch.

"Figueira is a big tourist destination. Beautiful beach. Many resorts. A casino. A good place for my sales, and not only at Christmas." said Leonor, pointing out the palatial homes along the river boulevard and the road with hotels fronting the wide, white sandy beach.

"They have surfing here," Adrienne added. "Jake would like it."

"Oh, there are better surfing beaches than this," said Leonor, gesturing to the south. "Coxos and Nazaré. My son-in-law Rodrigo goes there."

After lunch, they drove the coast-hugging road back toward Aveiro for more deliveries, and for fun, took a ferry across the bay to São Jacinto. They stopped to walk the dunes in the natural reserve there, the smell of the pines growing in the sand intoxicating. The wind was picking up, so they did not stay long but enjoyed the break before the last leg of the trip home through Ovar to show Andy the Válega Church with its fabled painted tile facade, shining in the setting sun of the late afternoon.

"I'm thrilled we got all the deliveries done. *Obrigada! Obrigada*! Thank you so much for the help. I could not have done it without you." Leonor spread her arms wide to encompass them both in a hug.

"We were happy to do it, and what a special way for Andy to see more of the countryside," Adrienne said, then added with a nod to the sky, "It looks like a storm coming in. I hope it won't rain on Christmas Eve. We're looking forward to seeing the *presépio* next to the church. Nativity scenes are a common part of our celebrations in America."

Sure enough, wind and rain blew in overnight. Adrienne and Andy bent low in their hooded jackets for the walk to Doroteia's where cookie baking was already underway. They spent a good three hours helping with the project. Rehe was carefully following his mother's instructions for mixing the batter and Adrienne, after a somewhat shaky beginning, proved adept at shaping the *biscoitos*. Andy, Dinis and the youngest, Eva, were in charge of the icing and dipping the cookies in red- and green-colored sugar.

"Don't sugar all of them," called Doroteia. "Your father and I like them plain."

She was making *Bolo Rei,* a ring-shaped cake made with dried fruits and nuts. "We eat this throughout the holiday, but it is tradition to serve it on January sixth. That's the twelfth day of Christmas, what we call King's Day or *Dia de Reis*." Adrienne and Andy watched as she tucked a fava bean into the dough, along with a coin. "Whoever gets the slice with the bean or the coin will have good luck all year. As long as they don't break a tooth on the coin!" she laughed.

They left as the children were arranging figures in moss they had collected for the nativity scene sitting by their tree. Doroteia placed a large shoe for each child by the fireplace, which she explained were to hold their presents. "Only if they have been good!"

On the way home, they ran into Lourenço who invited them to a post-Christmas party. "My daughter and her family are coming for Christmas and staying for the weekend. It will be a madhouse with the grandchildren, but I thought it would be fun to have people come by. I haven't had many guests since I moved home. It will be on Sunday afternoon as they head back to Porto on Monday morning."

The storm blew itself out and although it was not clear, there was no rain and as midnight approached the *praça* filled, people gathering by the tree at the church. Adrienne and Andy traded *Feliz Natal* greetings and people asked about their *Consoada,* their Christmas Eve supper. Adrienne acknowledged her attempt to make the traditional cod fish, potato and green vegetable dish and a pork roast which had been Andy's favorite part of the meal.

The church doors opened, welcoming everyone to the midnight mass. Adrienne and Andy joined the others for the *Missa do Galo,* Mass of the Rooster service. They watched as people lined up to kiss a portrait of baby Jesus and followed the group back outside to place the portrait in the *presépio* in the square and gather around the now-roaring bonfire. As they wandered home, they reminisced about early childhood holidays, mostly remembering their mother's beautiful decorations and the package opening by the Christmas tree. And their father's famously rich eggnog served on New Year's Day, which they had been too young to sample, except on the sly.

The next day was a quiet one. Despite invitations from Leonor and from Doroteia, Adrienne had wanted both Christmas Eve and Christmas Day meals to be for the two of them. They lingered over coffee and their version of *rabanadas,* a French toast-like dish often eaten for dessert. They had decided it made for the perfect breakfast treat. Gift-opening was simple—Andy had brought a soft wool sweater for Adrienne and she had found three vintage *azulejos* for him, thinking the tiles for which Portugal was famous would be a nice remembrance of his trip.

"I thought you might frame them. Maybe for your kitchen or the wall by your front door. Brighten up that house of yours!"

The remainder of the day was spent preparing and cooking the stuffed turkey, which they had been surprised to learn was also a traditional Christmas Day meal in Portugal. They took advantage of the improved weather and went out on the terrace with blankets and sipped wine while the turkey finished cooking. Andy sat back, stretched his legs out in front of him, and began to sing carols—usually only the first few lines before he forgot the words and had to start a new one.

The good weather continued the next morning and they walked another route into the hills to watch the sun break apart the clouds and feel it warm the day. Adrienne pointed out the farms where Leonor would be getting her herbs and the new signs for different trails and destinations.

"This is one of the projects I helped with before I left last summer," she said. "There are a couple of boys in town, young men really, who are hiking and biking enthusiasts. Doroteia's nephew Aldo is one of them. They want to make Veredas a jumping-off point for a trekking circuit. We talked about several ways to get started with advertising and establishing name recognition. This was one of them."

"It's a great idea. These hills are perfect for biking. I'd love to do it myself." He ran his hand approvingly over the sign. "They did a nice job on these. They look so professional."

"Lourenço helped Aldo and his friends design them and let the boys use his workshop to build them. He even provided the wood."

Further up in the hills they walked beside a vast vineyard, spreading as far as they could see into the valley. Adrienne pointed toward the Oliveira winery in the distance with its imposing stone house at the top of a winding drive. She shared the story of Nicholau and Lourenço skipping school to see the visiting Carmen Miranda.

"She was a friend of the Oliveira family, I guess. Apparently, they crept through the grapevines alongside the road and waited for her to drive by," Adrienne laughed.

"Pretty impressive place!" said Andy.

"The main house is now a small hotel. Very refined, I hear. There's a restaurant for the guests. But only for the guests. Very elegant."

"Maybe we should go spend the night, to try it out. And have a fancy dinner. But we're running out of time. I only have a few more days."

"And I wanted to take you inland to see some of the mountain country. I haven't been there myself. Plus at least a day in Lisbon. You haven't seen it at all!"

"I guess I'll have to come back!"

"I hope so. This has been so much fun. I've so enjoyed showing you my new life." Adrienne reached out to rest a hand on his arm, meaning every word.

≈≈≈≈≈≈≈

Adrienne was moving from the kitchen to the living room and back, considering what she might take to Lourenço's party. *Something to add to the table? There's sure to be a lot of food already.*

Something for him? No, too personal. He hadn't given her a Christmas present. And she'd already given him a housewarming gift.

"What are you fussing about?" asked Andy as he watched her pace.

"I want to take something to Lourenço's, but I can't decide what it should be. There's likely to be lots of food. And I'm not sure a gift is appropriate. I gave him a housewarming gift when he moved back home, so... I don't know."

"You like him," Andy looked closely at her as he said it.

She straightened, "Yes, I do. It kind of crept up on me. He wasn't the reason I came back, but I did think about him when I was in Brunswick packing up. Wondering what he'd think about my moving back here."

"He's clearly attracted to you."

"No... well... attracted? I'm not sure about that." She cocked her head at Andy. "He was happy when I returned. And pleased with the news I was back to stay. But, attracted? I don't know."

He pulled his hair back from his brow and peered intently at her. "Trust me. I can see it when he talks with you. My protective brother eyes, I guess."

Chapter 12: *The Party*

Adrienne had settled on some candy purchased in Figueira as the gift to take to Lourenço's. She knew it would not go to waste, despite as she saw on entering his house, an array of desserts on the sideboard.

"Feliz Natal!" said Lourenço, greeting her with a small hug and Andy with an eager handshake. He was dressed up, beaming. A grin on his rugged face and eyes alight. "Please, come meet my family."

He took them through the living room where a small crowd was chatting and sipping wine. "Here. This is my daughter Ana and her husband Fernao."

Without hesitation, Ana step forward and gave Adrienne a warm hug. She pulled back a little and in precise English said, "I have wanted to meet you." She leaned in again and whispered in Adrienne's ear, "It is you who helped my father come home. I cannot tell you how much I thank you."

Adrienne began to shake her head, but Ana nodded and said, "*Sim,* it is true."

Lourenço was looking at the two of them quizzically, then remembered himself and continued the introductions to Andy, remarking that Fernao was also in the computer business. "Quite new in Portugal," he said. "Fernao is with one of the few companies in Porto."

As he stepped away to greet new arrivals, Fernao and Andy began at once to talk about the world opening up through computers and the internet. Adrienne could see Andy's pleasure in finding a kindred spirit.

"Always it goes this way," sighed Ana. "Computer men! We may as well go and get wine."

As they made their way across the room, Adrienne stopped to exchange *Feliz Natals* with almost every small grouping. When she made it to the sideboard, Ana was holding out a glass of wine.

"You know everyone!" she smiled. "*Papai* said you had made a home here. Made many friends. Became part of Veredas."

"People have been so kind, so welcoming," Adrienne said. "They have made me feel a part of the community."

"*Não, não*. More. You have helped people. Helped with the businesses. Like Leonor. Like at the bakery. And I met the DeRosas. New here, but even Senhor DeRosa said your name when talking about changes at the school. You are tutoring."

Adrienne stood a little taller, "It sounds impressive when you say it that way. And it is flattering to hear people appreciate the little help I have given. It has been fun. And yes, allowed me to make friends here."

As she looked around the room, she noticed Leonor talking with an older couple she did not know. "Who is that talking with Leonor?"

"The Oliveiras. They own the winery in the valley."

"We walked by the vineyard and I showed Andy the house yesterday. Beautiful. Andy joked we should go spend a night there, so we could eat at the restaurant. I hear it is exquisite."

"*Papai* should take you! He knows them well and will not need to overnight for a good dinner."

Lourenço interrupted the chatter in the room with a cheerful, *"Meus amigos e minhas amigas! Feliz Natal!"*

He went on to thank people for coming and sharing his happiness at being back in his home. Then threw his arms out and invited people into the dining room where a buffet was laid out on the large table.

"You have all been so generous, adding so many delicious dishes to what we had prepared. Now you must eat—eat a lot!" Lourenço laughed as he pointed to the over-filled table. Platters of *bolinhos de bacalhau,* the famous cod fritters, and *linguiça* and other sausages, and tureens with *caçoila,* a marinated pork, stewed favas beans, plates of goat and sheep cheeses, and baskets of crusty rolls.

Throughout the evening Adrienne and Andy would reconnect, but they had no lack of people joining their conversations or drawing them away to introduce them to others. They all had to pantomime at times to bridge the lack of a shared language.

Ana and Fernao knew many of the younger people, friends of Ana's from past school years. They also knew Aldo and Tomás, the two friends who were avid bike riders and had made the signs for the trekking circuit. An involved conversation among the four men ensued. Adrienne drifted away to sit with Doroteia and Rehor, who were proudly watching their two boys refill platters on the buffet and clear away used plates and glasses. Lourenço had hired them to help out.

"And keep them out of trouble!" laughed Rehor. "They are getting to that age!"

"And Rehe helped with the cooking. He offered to pitch in when I was making some dishes to bring. I think he could be good at it."

The party went on into the evening with many bottles of wine opened and people visiting the buffet table time after time until they held up their hands to ward off Lourenço's attempts to fill their plates yet again. Ana returned to Adrienne's side to say they would be leaving in the morning but hoped her father would bring her to Porto for a visit.

"This has not been a good time to get to know you. Or for you to see much of my children. I would like that."

Adrienne assured her she would welcome the trip, saying she had not yet had the chance to see Porto. "And not much of Lisbon either. Only two days when I was first here last spring."

"Andy and Fernao like each other, I think," Ana said, pointing to the two of them looking out the tall windows toward the lights of town below.

"I think so, too. Similar interests. Not just the computer, but also biking. And I know he enjoyed meeting Aldo and Tomás. Andy was excited to hear about the idea of Veredas becoming part of a trekking circuit. Thought the terrain was perfect for it. I'm hoping it will be another reason he'll want to come back in the warmer weather."

They were getting ready to leave the party, saying their goodbyes. Andy was bubbling over with enthusiasm about the hiking and biking opportunities Veredas could provide. "I promised Aldo and Tomás I would help them. Fernao said he would, too, and we have a plan for communicating via computer when I get home. We also talked with Senhor Oliveira. He wants to update his winery—the recordkeeping anyway. I think he will hire Fernao!"

"Sounds like you made a bunch of new friends. Now you have to come back."

Andy beamed, "I plan to! And I want to bring Jake and Kathryn. I know Jake will want to try the surfing. And Kathryn will want to see the art."

"I would so love to have them. We haven't had time to see much on this trip, but we could plan a real vacation if the kids come."

"Why don't we head out tomorrow? To Lisbon. We could spend a couple of days there before I leave."

"That's a great idea. We can take the morning bus to Aveiro and the train from there."

"What's this about going to Lisbon? Taking a bus?" Lourenço came up behind them carrying two wine bottles. "Here, these are for you. I have many too many left over."

As Andy relieved him of the wine, Adrienne filled Lourenço in on their plan to spend a few days in Lisbon before Andy flew home.

"*Não, não*. You must let me drive you to Aveiro to the train. I will be up early to see the kids off anyway."

Despite their protests about the inconvenience, Lourenço insisted and bid them goodnight. They walked down the road with Leonor and Doroteia and Rehor, sharing the plan for the trip to Lisbon.

"We will miss you, Andy," said Leonor. "And I thank you for your help. It made for a fun adventure to deliver my goods. Which, by the way, I heard were big sellers over the holiday! I may have to give you a part of the proceeds." She waved goodbye and turned into her walkway.

"You must come back, Andy," said Doroteia. "You have inspired Aldo and Tomás. They are so excited. I heard them tonight encouraging my sister Benita to go ahead with her plan to turn her house into a *pensão* for the tourists they are sure will come."

"I knew she was considering it," said Adrienne. "Will she do it?"

"I think so," said Doroteia. "Maybe we can go see her when you come back from Lisbon. Help her with ideas about what to do."

There were hugs all around as they went their separate ways. Adrienne and Andy made their way home and said a quick goodnight as they each went to pack for their trip.

Chapter 13: *Lisbon*

With a hurried thanks and reassurance from Andy that he would return, Adrienne and Andy left Lourenço and boarded the train to Lisbon. Waving to him on the platform as they settled into their seats, they heaved a sigh of relief at having made the train.

"That was close," said Andy as the train pulled away. "Lourenço is a terrific guy, and a great tour guide, but the little side trip took longer than expected."

"He loves the art nouveau buildings on the *Rua João de Mendonça* and along the Central Canal," said Adrienne. "Wanted to make sure you saw them. I think he hopes you'll fall in love with Portugal like I have and come back again."

"As I said, I think he's sweet on you!" Andy grinned.

"So you say," and Adrienne, looking skeptical, then turned her gaze to the city streets giving way to terraced hillsides. Andy let her be, sitting back and sharing the view and the quiet. Her distant look made him think she was mulling over what he had said about Lourenço. He knew her to be a cautious person, rarely sure of herself or her decisions. He wanted to help, to be encouraging, but what was the right thing to do? Urge her to pursue a relationship with Lourenço, as that's what it seemed might be happening? Or wait, explore her new-found independence a while before making a commitment? He wasn't sure, so kept his peace.

They arrived in early afternoon at *Santa Apolónia* Station and followed directions Lourenço had given them to a small hotel a ten-minute walk away. Checked in and out on the street in no time, they wanted to start right in with the sightseeing they had planned on the way down. First, however, was a late lunch.

Following the advice of the concierge, Adrienne and Andy found themselves in a small tavern a few blocks from the hotel, known for *petisco,* something like Spanish tapas. They were served quickly, and Andy downed an icy cold beer with his *bifana,* marinated pork sandwich, and Adrienne a glass of white wine with her garlicky prawns.

It was not long before they were out the door and off into the historic neighborhood with many of Lisbon's most famous sites—the *Praça Luís de Camões,* a town square and meeting place, the city's oldest cathedral, and finally, the *São Jorge* Castle on a hillside reached via an elevator built after the turn of the century, called the *Santa Justa* Lift. Adrienne had seen all of this on her summer bus tour, but it had been so hurried she barely remembered. The slower, more thoughtful pace with Andy gave her a second chance to take in the beauty. As evening set in they wandered the mosaic-patterned cobbled streets with other tourists looking for dinner and a chance to hear *Fado,* the nostalgic guitar music popular throughout the country.

Checking the menu boards outside each restaurant door, they settled on one serving clams and the grilled octopus Andy wanted to try. Sipping a fresh white wine suggested by the waiter, they listened to a mournful singer.

"Sounds sad," said Andy.

"Yes," nodded Adrienne, swaying slightly with the music. "*Fado* often is. She's singing about a lover lost at sea. How she will always miss him."

They dove right in when dinner was served, and both were silent for a few minutes in appreciation of the food.

"This is heavenly," said Adrienne. "I'd never have thought of pork and clams together. Nicholau said to try it. That it is a favorite dish here in Lisbon."

"Can't be any better than this octopus. What did you call it?"

"*Polvo à lagareiro*. Doroteia told me it is a traditional Christmas-time dinner. *Lagareiro* means owner of an olive oil press, so I guess it is simply dressed with olive oil."

"Nothing simple about it. Absolutely delicious!"

They shared tastes of their dishes, drank their wine, and listened to the music, but left shortly as the day had been a long one and they wanted to make the best use of the next one. Their last full day together.

"We can start at the big market and have breakfast there. It will have *pastéis de nata*. I know you've had them, but there is a bakery here in Lisbon that is supposed to have been the first one to sell them. I'm not sure where it is, but I've no doubt they are served everywhere."

They started for the market but found they couldn't last the half-hour walk from the hotel, stopping at a bakery along the way, and at another overlooking the river before reaching their first destination. The day proceeded in the same manner—picking a place to visit and being waylaid by the sight of something else, a gift shop, or a tempting aroma drawing them in for lunch. It was a meander with several loops and some backtracking when they got lost in the tangle of streets. To give themselves a rest, they took a taxi across the bridge to the *Cristo Rei* to stand and gaze at the monument, and despite a cold wind, rode the elevator up for the stunning view of the city across the Tagus River.

Andy rested his hands on the railing. "This has been the most wonderful trip. I can't thank you enough for encouraging me to come."

"I loved having you! It has been so much fun. You have to tell the kids about it. And that I so hope they'll come visit in the summer."

"I'm sure they will. Especially if I pay!"

As they walked back to the hotel, Andy decided to risk bringing up what had been on his mind. "You know, I wondered what Veredas would be like, and how you fit there. How you were making a life for yourself there. I had a hard time picturing it. And now, having seen it—and you as part of it—it's so incredible. You are much more connected there than I imagined. And you seem different. Certainly happier, but also more... more adventurous, more... I don't know... " he laughed. "Out there!"

Adrienne laughed back, "Out there? Adventurous? I don't know about that."

"It's true. I see you exploring things, open to all kinds of possibilities I'm not sure you considered before. Maybe you never had the opportunity. Maybe you were always like this, but just couldn't get there. I hope… " he stopped.

"Hope what?"

"That you keep going. Wherever it leads." He stopped again, and seeing Adrienne's smile, decided he would leave it at that.

But Adrienne's smile was hiding a sudden anxiety about "wherever it leads" and wondering herself what it really meant. She lay awake that night considering it.

The next morning, having packed and left their bags with the concierge, they headed to the National Museum of Contemporary Art.

"Kathryn won't forgive me if I miss this. She read up on it when I told her I was coming to Portugal. It was refurbished a couple of years ago and has been trying to develop its collection as well. She said it would be a chance to see a museum in the process of trying to re-define itself as a showcase for contemporary Portuguese art and artists. She was pretty excited about it."

"Maybe you can bring her something from the gift shop. You said you hadn't found the right present for her."

"I was hoping we'd have the chance. Maybe a book about the restoration effort. I think she'd like that."

The brief visit allowed them to see some of the museum's permanent collection and one of the current exhibitions. "I wish we had more time, but we'd better go if I'm to make my plane. And you'll be able to catch a train and be back in Veredas before dark."

As they walked back to retrieve their bags, Adrienne lamented the short time they had had in Lisbon. "I'm sorry we didn't spend more of your time here. There's so much to see. And other places as well. Next time… "

She took Andy's arm and said seriously, "I want you to know how much your being here matters to me. Sharing this new life I've started. I thought about what you said… wherever it leads. I don't know if I always wanted something like this. I don't think so. I don't think I could have imagined it. I ask myself every other day what I'm doing here, and there is no answer. So, I just keep going."

"Sounds like the right answer to me. You can't know what's ahead. So, why not keep going?"

As she looked out at the hills on her way home, Adrienne pondered Andy's thoughts, vacillating between the truth of them and the unease that truth triggered in her.

Chapter 14: *Winter*

January and February were quiet, somewhat of a relief to Adrienne after the nonstop activity in December, but the months sped by. She helped Leonor with her business and worked with Doroteia's sister Benita and her son on their plans for the *pensão*.

Aldo was the one with ideas about how to attract hikers and bicyclists to the guesthouse and proved to be quite an artist with his sketches of the birds, butterflies, and plants to be included in the advertising. Benita, on the other hand, was more concerned about the accommodations and how to turn the small rooms in her house into comfortable bedrooms for her guests. She and Doroteia tried different combinations of beds, tables, and chairs, with Rehe and Dinis moving the furniture from room to room. Adrienne suggested that Benita sleep a night in each room to see exactly what worked and what did not, what was missing, what would make it nicer. By the time she had finished, Benita had all but emptied Doroteia's shop of lamps and small rugs.

This was not the only activity in Veredas during the winter months, all driven by the hoped-for growth of business. The grocery store was finishing the installation of the ice cream counter and the bar on the edge of the village was building an outdoor eating space with a large pizza oven—providing work for Lourenço and for Aldo and Tomás, both of whom he had taken on part-time in the carpentry workshop. And with the addition of the coffee shop, the bakery had hired an apprentice,

Marcos, who came from a village in the hills to the east. Born into a large family who ran a dairy, he fit right in with the early morning schedule the bakery demanded and was thrilled to have his own small room above the shop—a first for the young man who had always shared bedrooms, and sometimes beds, with his three brothers.

The other news was the imminent sale of the pharmacy. The aging pharmacist had conceded it was time and his son had found a new job, so the entire family living above the shop would be moving—the pharmacist and his wife to a small cottage close by and the son's family to Porto. Although they were still in negotiations, the new owners were generating excitement in town. The incoming pharmacist's wife was trained as a Physician's Assistant. For the first time in its history, Veredas might have a local source of medical care.

"I know it's too soon to count on it, but I can't help but hope it works out," Leonor said. "Making the trip to Aveiro isn't a terribly long drive, but it will be so much more convenient to have someone here in town. And it will be a comfort knowing someone would be available in an emergency."

"It was Doroteia's first thought, too," Adrienne nodded. "She told me about Rehe's fall from a tree a few years ago. It turned out okay, but the time it took to get him to the hospital was frightening for her."

"I haven't gotten the details, but I understand both the pharmacist and his wife are interested in herbal remedies."

"Maybe the pharmacy will be a new outlet for your business!"

"I know! It's good I have Carolina. I didn't expect my little hobby to grow into such a big effort. It is almost more than I can manage."

Adrienne leaned across the table and shook a finger at Leonor. "I told you it could be a success. Be careful what you ask for."

"I know, I know. Isn't that what you said when I first began to get the orders… when I crowed about having more money than I knew what to do with!"

"You've worked hard. It has been an inspiration to other people in town. I'm sure it's behind some of the changes we've seen in the last few months."

Leonor shrugged, "Maybe. But people have been worrying about the village dying for some time. You see the shops that have been shuttered for years. The young men and women moving away to get jobs. Or for more excitement. We have all talked about ways to make change, to make things better. I was just the first to try something. Out of boredom!"

"And look at you now."

"Don't forget. You played a big role in making it happen. I thank you! *Obrigada!*"

Adrienne was smiling as she walked toward home. Even more so when meeting Lourenço on his way to his house. The invitation to dinner at Nicholau's was welcome. She had heard a rumor about Marissa and hoped to find out if there was any truth to it.

"Now, Marissa," she said as she made her way to the table that evening, "I heard you are seeing the apprentice at the bakery. Is it true?"

Marissa nodded, "*Sim,* Marcos and I have gone out together. Well, we met for coffee at the bakery café. And he is coming to dinner at the house. To meet my parents."

"And... " Adrienne raised her eyebrows.

Marissa smiled shyly. "We'll see."

When Marissa left with their order, Lourenço leaned over and said quietly, "I hear it is going well. At least that's what Aldo and Tomás say. It's a good thing. New people don't come to town often." He stopped, then said, "Well, up until recently."

Adrienne chuckled, "Yes, I guess I started a trend."

"It's true. First you, then the DeRosas, then Marcos, and soon the new pharmacist and his wife."

"I imagine it is hard for young people here. Why they tend to go elsewhere."

"Yes, true for my Ana. Who, by the way, is asking if we will visit. Would you be interested in a trip to Porto next week?" Lourenço fidgeted with his silverware, unsure of her answer. Adrienne was smiling, a secretive little smile.

"What? Is there something about going to Porto that is especially amusing?"

She ducked her head, feeling shy about it, "Well… it will be my birthday. March 12th."

"What! And you were not going to tell me? But we must celebrate. You absolutely must come."

"No, please. I'd love to come to Porto, but nothing special. I don't want a fuss."

Lourenço shook his head vigorously, "Ana will not forgive me if we visited and let it pass."

The remainder of the evening was spent planning the excursion. Preparing for bed Adrienne, she found herself thinking not about the trip to Porto but how Lourenço's initial grizzled appearance and gruff demeanor had hidden not only a warm, caring nature but a good-looking man—a strong face, lively eyes, a touch of gray at his temples. She caught herself picturing the two of them together. *Is it possible?* she asked herself. *Was Andy right about Lourenço's feelings for her? Is that what she wanted?* She wasn't sure but decided to follow Andy's suggestion to just keep going.

Chapter 15: *Porto*

Lourenço had chosen a smaller back road to Porto rather than the shorter trip via the highway, allowing them to enter the city from the east along the Douro River. They had taken the winding bends slowly as it had rained early in the day, but the cloud cover was breaking up as they headed down and Adrienne stared at the beauty of the terraced hillsides below and around them. They were not yet showing the green of spring but were lush just the same. The river curved away from the unending fields of grapevines as the view to the city opened ahead of them.

"*Belo, não*?" said Lourenço.

"*Sim, sim,*" responded Adrienne. "*Tão bonito,* so beautiful."

"We can stop and sample the port, but it is more fun to go during harvest. More to see."

"And Ana is expecting us."

They crossed the river into the historic downtown as Lourenço wanted Adrienne to see the colors in the afternoon light. Going slowly up the old steep streets, the fading stucco of the buildings in blue, yellow, green, and brown set off the red tiles of the roofs. Adrienne was enchanted with the blue and white decorative tiles everywhere, sharing that she had given some to Andy for Christmas.

As they pulled their bags from the car, they were surrounded by Lourenço's grandchildren— João, the oldest at age eight, and Inês, a few years younger. Ana stood in the doorway with the toddler on her hip, Gabriela.

"Olá, Papai. And welcome! *Bem vinda,* Adrienne," Ana called. Inês wrapped herself around her grandfather's leg and clung to it as he stumped his way up the walk to the door, praising João as he did so for carrying Adrienne's bag. There was a flurry of hugs and jostling as Adrienne was escorted to João's room, which he proudly reported was to be hers as he would share with his sisters.

"Meu avô vai dormir na sofá," he crowed and pointed to the couch in the living room where Lourenço was to sleep. There were more hugs all around as Fernao arrived and the entire tribe moved to the kitchen for the final steps to finish the dinner Ana had prepared.

Ana had made *porco preto* for Adrienne's birthday, a succulent black ham from pigs raised in the south of Portugal. And for dessert, *bolo de bolacha e caramelo,* a cake made of wafers and caramel. The children had insisted as it was their favorite, always requested on their birthdays. As it was served, the older two stood on either side of Adrienne and sang Happy Birthday in English, having practiced all week for the occasion.

After the children had been read to by Lourenço and were settled, the four adults gathered in the living room, thankful for the peace and another glass of wine. Fernao relaxed back into his chair and talked about his recent conversation with Andy, their shared excitement about the growing capabilities of the internet and the ease of communication between America and Portugal.

"He also said he planned to bring his children to Veredas in the summer. Jake... yes?" Fernao asked. "Jake is already reading about Portuguese history. And looking up everything he can find about surfing beaches. I told Andy to let him know we have friends who surf. They can tell us where."

Lourenço added, "Rodrigo, Leonor's son-in-law, also surfs, doesn't he?"

"*Sim,* at Nazaré," said Ana. "His parents have a house there. He and Valera go often."

"Andy says Kathryn is excited about seeing the art," said Fernao. "Especially the contemporary art."

"Yes," Adrienne nodded, "when we were in Lisbon Andy and I went to the National Museum of Contemporary Art. He said she would certainly want to go there."

"She will also want to see the Serralves, here in Porto," said Ana. "If she can! It has been under construction since 1991. I will try to find out when they expect to open. I think it may be soon. But the building itself is worth seeing—part of a large park with traditional gardens, beautiful woods, a farm. We can take a drive there tomorrow. The children love the park."

"It sounds as if there many things to see," said Adrienne. "Where else will we go?"

The remainder of the evening was spent in spirited discussion of places to visit, where to have lunch, and things Adrienne should not miss on her first trip to Porto.

≈≈≈≈≈≈≈

On the drive back to Veredas on Sunday afternoon, Lourenço asked about her favorites among the things they had done.

Without hesitation, Adrienne answered, "My birthday dinner. Thank you. I would have let the day pass, but I am glad we didn't. It was very special."

"One should never ignore a birthday, especially as we grow older. It is what my father said. One never knows how many more there will be to celebrate." He reached over and patted her hand. "You will have many more, I'm sure. What else did you like?"

"The walk and the trolley ride through the old part of the town," she answered. "It was beautiful. The *azulejo* tiles everywhere, on every building it seemed. And playing with the children in the park, at Serralves. It was their favorite, I am sure."

They talked more about where they had gone and how they thought both Jake and Kathryn would find things of interest in Porto. It felt like a growing city, full of life. Certainly one of the places to put on the list for the summer visit. Aside from Andy and Fernao likely wanting to see each other in person.

Adrienne studied the passing countryside. "I wonder if I should buy a car. I think we'll need it when Andy and the kids are here."

"I'm sure you could borrow a car, from Leonor, from me."

"I have been considering it anyway," Adrienne said. "The bus isn't always convenient and although Leonor has been so kind to lend me hers, I don't want to impose."

"I would be happy to help with the search for one, but I think Rehor is the man to ask. He probably has a better feel for where to look, where to get a good deal. Remember there will be taxes. And insurance, too. Are you sure renting a car wouldn't be better?"

Except for agreeing on the rent she paid him, Lourenço had never talked with Adrienne about her financial circumstances. On the trip up and now this drive back, they had moved beyond small talk and the out-the-window observances, discussing different people in Veredas and his family's relationship to them or how he had come to know them growing up. But Lourenço was unsure if he was prying.

"It just occurred to me that the car might be an expense you don't want to take on," he finally said.

Adrienne shook her head, "No, money is not a problem. Living in Veredas is less expensive than it would be for me in the States. Arthur left me in good shape and my house sold for more than I expected."

"Was it difficult to sell your house? You said you loved the garden, but I can't remember you saying much about the house."

"No. Not hard at all. I had lived there many years, but somehow, didn't feel attached to it. The garden, yes. That was different. It was harder to leave."

"It is hard for me to imagine. I am the fourth generation living in my house. The fourth generation of woodworkers. Each one adding something to make it his own."

"What did you add? You didn't tell me when you showed me around the first time."

"There has always been a back porch, but I expanded it and added the railings and screens. My grandmother and mother had grown flowers and vegetables in the backyard, but Jacolin loved gardening and made it into something much more beautiful, more special. We would often sit on the porch in the evening admiring it." He quieted, then went on, "While I can't say I've done much more than tidy the garden, I still enjoy bundling up on a crisp evening and having a glass of wine there. My parents are also buried in the garden."

"Really? I would have thought they'd be in the cemetery beside the church."

Lourenço laughed, "*Não*. My father had an argument with the *sacerdote,* the padre. It was when I was very young and I never learned much about it, but my mother said she had begged him to make it right, to settle it. There was gossip in town and she was embarrassed. But he refused. Never went to church again. So, when he died, she knew he wouldn't want to be buried there. We buried him in the garden. And before she died, she asked me to bury her alongside him. So, I did."

"And Jacolin?" Adrienne asked.

"She is in the cemetery. Where she wanted to be, near her parents." He went on to share the close relationship between his wife and her parents, who had had no other children.

"Oh, look at me—*falar pelos cotovelos!*" Lourenço shook his head.

"Speak with the elbows? What does that mean?" Adrienne asked, confused by the nonsensical phrase.

"It means I talk too much!"

"But I am enjoying hearing about your family and people in Veredas. I have been wanting to ask about Rehor's and Leonor's fathers. You said there was a story about them and how their names came to be on the *placa* in the square."

Lourenço started in, "It is a long story... " stopped to collect his thoughts, then began again. "You know during World War II Portugal was neutral. It meant countries from both sides were active here. Countries allied with the Germans and those fighting against them. And that people escaping from Germany and occupied France, refugees, came here looking to get away. To get to America or anywhere. Many were Jews, not all. But the police—the *Policia de Vigilancia e de Defense do Estado,* state surveillance police—were sure there would be communists, fleeing Nazis, political enemies of Portugal, too. So, it was dangerous. For the refugees and for anyone helping them.

"My father... he loved the mountains. Have I told you? We often went hiking and climbing in the east when I was a boy. Anyway, Rehor and Leonor's fathers, who also hiked, went to help people make it over the mountains. Not in Portugal, but in northern Spain, the Pyrenees. They would get them through the mountains, then west, and hand them off to others who would take them to Lisbon—others, including my father. *Pai* did not go with them into the mountains. I don't know exactly why. He never said. Perhaps my grandfather forbade it. Worried about his son's safety or that the police would arrest him."

"Arrest him for what?" asked Adrienne.

"For creating a problem between Portugal and the Nazis. Or between Portugal and Spain, who was also neutral, but friendlier to Germany and to Italy. To be caught in Spain helping refugees could put Portugal in a difficult situation.

"So, *Pai* would meet Rehor or Leonor's father at the border and help people get to Lisbon, where transport out of Europe was possible. This went on for a good while. Anyway, although no one learned the details, a group in the mountains was killed in 1942, Rehor and Leonor's fathers among them. Maybe it was the *Policia,* thinking there were criminals among the refugees. Maybe men involved in smuggling, which was also fairly common at the time. Maybe a spy in the underground network who set up an ambush. No one knew.

"They were not the only men Veredas lost during the war. But the plaque with all the names was not put up until 1969. After Salazar stepped down. The government had never pursued many of the deaths occurring during the war and made it known they considered some of them suspicious. The people in the village waited until the new government was installed and then had the plaque made."

The story finished, they were both quiet as Lourenço drove the last few kilometers to town until Adrienne sighed heavily and said, "It must have been difficult. Not knowing what happened. Leonor has never talked about it."

"Maybe her mother didn't want to talk about it. I know my father didn't. He felt guilty, I think. I knew Rehor and Leonor's fathers had died in Spain during the war, shortly after we were all born, but not much more than that. It wasn't until they hung the plaque that *Pai* told me the story. About successful trips, but also close calls and times things didn't work out so well. I remember thinking, no wonder *Pai* doesn't want to talk about it. Why he was especially attentive to Rehor, always including him in our outings to the mountains, always suggesting we share holiday meals with his family and with Leonor's. And why he was sad sometimes and would go to the workshop and shoo me away or go to the attic and close the door."

"It must have been hard."

"*Sim*, I wanted to… I don't know, comfort him, I guess. And I couldn't. My mother either. She said we had to be patient and it would pass."

"I never knew much about refugees escaping through Portugal. Not much beyond what was in the movie, Casablanca." Adrienne shook her head, "We don't go deeply into history in our schools, and certainly not much about Portugal, except that it was neutral during World War II."

"The war played out here in Europe, so it would be given more attention here."

"Yes, it's true. But what you've told me makes me want to learn more. Makes me realize how little I know about Portugal's history or its literature. I studied literature in college, but hardly anything from Portugal."

"Oh, we have many writers you might like. I have some in my library. Eça de Queirós and Fernando Pessoa and José Saramago."

"I would like to. I read one of Saramago's books, Blindness, but nothing by the others you mentioned."

Arriving in Veredas, Lourenço drove to Adrienne's apartment and unloaded her bag. As he carried it up the stairs, she said, "Thank you for such good conversation on the way home. It has given me something to think about and something new to learn about Portugal. And thank you for taking me to Porto. I so enjoyed the trip. Seeing the town, seeing Ana and Fernao and the children. Celebrating my birthday. Everything."

Setting down her bag, Lourenço waited while she unlocked the door. When she turned back, he bent and gave her a brief kiss. She was momentarily startled but returned it with one of her own.

Chapter 16: *Coming Together*

Adrienne thought about the kiss as she unpacked and made dinner. She wondered if Lourenço was thinking of it as well. *Was it anything more than a friendly acknowledgment of a weekend of fun? A parting birthday wish? I know he likes me, but what would that mean?* She shook her head as she crawled into bed. *And what do I want it to mean?*

She did not exactly avoid seeing Lourenço the next day, but somehow made sure she was busy visiting Leonor and Doroteia to tell them of the trip and checking in with Benita about her progress on the guesthouse. She had not planned to go to Pap'açorda's, but as evening rolled around, she found herself uninterested in cooking. When Adrienne walked into the restaurant, there he was, sitting and talking with Marissa.

Lourenço stood and held out a chair for her. She suddenly felt shy, dipping her head a bit as she sat and then engaging Marissa in conversation about the dinner special. Her voice trailed off with an *obrigada* as Marissa turned for the kitchen. Adrienne looked over at Lourenço. He was smiling and holding out a book to her.

"*Livro do Desassossego*, Book of Disquiet, by Bernardo Soares, a name used by Fernando Pessoa. I think you might like it." He laughed and went on, "It is in Portuguese, so it may take you some time to make your way through it."

"I will put my dictionary to good use. Thank you."

He leaned forward, elbows on the table. "I thought about our trip all day today. What fun it was. We travel well together.

We should do more. There is much of the country you have not seen. The mountains to the east and the area south of Lisbon, although it is full of tourists most of the year. Maybe the Azores. It is volcanic and… "

He stopped. "There I go again— *falar pelos cotovelos*!"

Adrienne grinned and said, "*Não,* I like it when you are excited about something you want to tell me. I can almost see how you must have been as a boy."

Lourenço was about to respond but stopped when Nicholau brought out the wine and sat down to hear about their travels. The conversation turned to the drive, the things they had seen in Porto, and the family. As dinner arrived, the moment seemed lost and unfinished.

But as he walked her home Lourenço took her hand. "What I wanted to say before was that I am happy when I have a chance to share something with you. It has been a long time since I have felt so good."

She drew a breath and slowly said, "And it is a long time for me as well. As I told you, my husband and I were not so close. Especially in the last years of his life."

She went silent and Lourenço tightened his hand around hers.

It was a few days before they saw one another again. Lourenço's dropping by the apartment and greeting her with a kiss felt comfortable and uncomplicated. The offered glass of wine turned into two as they talked about the book he had given her and whether she was enjoying it. As he stood in the doorway to leave, what began as a simple kiss goodnight became something quite different. Soft and sweet grew into a deeper searching. A tentative flickering of tongues caused their breaths to catch and they drew back, looking into each other's eyes.

"Boa noite," said Lourenço.

Adrienne closed the door behind him and leaned against it, savoring the lingering sensation on her lips and her feeling of surprise. For his part, Lourenço could not help grinning as he made his way home.

When they met in the square a few days later, neither shied away. Each reaching for the other's hand, dropping it as they realized people were milling about in the first Saturday afternoon market of the year. They tried to be casual as they strolled together from stall to stall, eyeing the early vegetables and talking with the vendors, but the air felt charged between them. When they ran into Doroteia and Rehor it was with a sense of relief that they drew away from each other, Adrienne engaging Doroteia in conversation about her sister's *pensão* and Rehor telling Lourenço about an incident on his bus route the day before. A dinner invitation was accepted and the easy banter around the table with the family lessened the heightened awareness they shared.

They had not walked more than a block toward Adrienne's apartment when Lourenço took her arm and pulled her into an empty side street. He put his arms around her, leaned down and took her lips with his. Gentle, long and luscious. They parted with a sigh, her head resting on his chest. She could feel his heart beating. Matching her own.

"*Ai meu Deus,*" he breathed into her hair.

"My feeling as well," Adrienne said, looking up at him.

Lourenço exhaled audibly, "We should go slowly."

She sighed again, took his hand, and they walked back into the light of the main street.

When Lourenço came to her door with flowers the following afternoon she was not surprised. She had been thinking of him since they parted—hoping he would appear, then that he would not, then hoping again.

His face was gentle, serious. "Just talking. It is a good idea, don't you think?"

Adrienne nodded, took the flowers, and beckoned him in. Lourenço sat on the couch, looking at the floor.

"I don't know… it's been a long while… I… "

"I don't know either," she said. "I want…" *What do I want?* There was no question in her mind about what she wanted. On that she was clear. She was aching for him. It was what it would lead to, where it might go that was making her hesitate.

"I guess I'm afraid—afraid this will change things."

"It will change things," Lourenço said. "Of that I am sure. The question is, do we want them to change? Do you want them to change?"

"Do you?"

"I think, yes. *Sim,*" he said firmly. He looked closely at her, trying to read the effect of those words and whether her answer would be the same. He saw her eyes widen, a flicker of worry, and a small, shy smile. All within a matter of seconds.

Emboldened, he went on, "We do not know what will happen. But we are not youngsters. We are two adults, each with some years and some experience behind us. We have pasts. We have had other people in our lives. I was up most of the night wrestling with this. I know your marriage with Arthur was different than mine with Jacolin, but I have no fears she would disapprove."

His speech was halted by an eruption of laughter from Adrienne. She tried to stifle it but could not and struggled to get the words out, "I am sorry. *Sinto muito.* I can't help it. Arthur and what he would think is the furthest thing from my mind."

Lourenço sat back and said, "So what is on your mind?"

"Você," she said. "You." She stopped, took a breath, and knelt before him, her hands on his knees. "I do know what I am feeling, and it is excitement. It is a long time since I have felt it. A very long time. But I remember—excitement and anticipation. Those are the feelings of my body and my heart. What I wrestled with in the night was in my mind. What if we begin and find those feelings change? How will we feel in time? And… "

Adrienne's eyes overflowed, tears running down her cheeks. Lourenço reached out, but she held up a hand. "And if we decide it is not right for us to be together... What then? What will we do? Will I have to leave Veredas?"

There, she had said it. She rocked back on her heels and hid her face in her hands, sobbing now. Lourenço took her hands in his, pulling her into his lap, stroking her hair, letting her cry. Slowly the tears gave way to hiccups, then silence.

"Minha Querida," Lourenço said softly, kissing the top of her head. "We would not let that happen. I would not let that happen. However it turns out, we will find a way to make things work. You have found yourself here. I could not ever take that from you." His hands moved to her face, forcing her to look him in the eye. "You must believe this."

"I want to. I do." Adrienne began to cry again. "It's just... what I said sounds... I don't know... petty, trivial, *mesquinha,* is that the right word?"

Lourenço put a finger to her lips, but she shook her head. "I mean, we are talking about caring for one another, coming together, a relationship. And all I can think about is whether I might have to go back to New Jersey!" The last coming out as a shriek.

Lourenço hugged her to him, slid her from his lap, and said, *"Venha,* come."

He led her to the bedroom and slowly undressed her, then himself. They lay face to face, taking in one another's shyness, anticipation, wonder. Tender beginnings rapidly became hungry. Lips and hands searching, finding. Carefully paced, with intentions to go slowly soon overcome by appetites held too long in check.

Chapter 17: *Revealing*

In the days that followed, Adrienne and Lourenço were circumspect about their growing relationship. At least they thought so. Lourenço would leave early if he had spent the night. The two would greet one another on the street with warmth and a brief hug, but no kiss. The occasional dinners at Pap'açorda's were unchanged, sipping a glass of wine with Nicholau and teasing Marissa about Marcos and their plans.

It was Leonor who hinted their secret was no secret. "You are happy, Adrienne. *Não?*"

Adrienne looked up from her cup of coffee, saying slowly, "*Sim,* I am."

"That is good. We are happy for you."

"We?"

"Oh, me. Doroteia. Rehor. Benita. Carolina."

Adrienne laughed. "So, everyone knows?"

"*Claro,* of course. This is a small town. People notice. They talk. But it is friendly gossip. Everyone likes you. They see Lourenço is a happier man. And everyone thinks he has been alone too long." She hugged her friend and added, "Jacolin would be happy, too."

When Adrienne ran into Doroteia later, looking up at the tall woman with a stern expression. She began with, "OK, when were you going to say something to me?"

"I figured you would tell us when you were ready. I told Rehor to say nothing to Lourenço. To let him come to us. I think it's killing him to keep quiet."

"Well, he might as well go ahead. It looks like everyone in town knows."

Adrienne turned the thought over in her mind as she walked home. *So, what does it mean that everyone knows?* More importantly, *that they think Lourenço has been alone long enough*. It had been a long time for him. Six years now. But for her, less than two, and in coming to Veredas she had found a new and unfamiliar sense of freedom and independence. As she climbed the stairs to her apartment, she shook herself. *It's not like he's asked me to marry him or anything. Nothing has changed. I'm still here in my own place, on my own.*

Yet, things had changed. How much was still a question.

Lourenço's face that evening, when he came to pick her up for dinner, alternated between amusement and irritation. "Seems everyone in town knows. Rehor told me. Said he'd known for a while."

"I know. I talked with both Doroteia and Leonor today. I guess we should have known it wouldn't be a secret for long."

Lourenço heaved a huge sigh. "I know, I know. I hoped we would have a little more time to get used to the idea ourselves. To enjoy that we had a secret."

When they sat down at Pap'açorda's and Nicholau bustled over to greet them, Lourenço adopted a fierce stare and said, "I suppose you know, too."

"Meu amigo, certamente! How could I not? You are my friends. I see you. I know." And with that, he disappeared into the back and returned with a bottle. "A special *brut espumante,* sparkling brut from Caves São João, not far to the south of us," he showed Adrienne the label.

Raising his glass to them in a salute. *"Saude! Estou feliz por voce.* I am happy for you."

As if the new relationship and its exposure around Veredas were not enough, Adrienne read a note from Andy a few days later with some concern. *Oh no, Andy and the kids are coming. What will I tell them?* Then she smiled, realizing they, too, would be happy for her. She raced up the road to Lourenço's house, knocking impatiently and poking her head in his back door.

"Lourenço! Onde você está? Where are you?" As he appeared in the kitchen, she waved the postcard and panted out, "It's from Andy. He's coming and bringing Kathryn and Jake. They'll be here in two months."

"Oh my, more people to explain to." His brow furrowed. "Will Andy be happy… about us?"

"I think so. He told me you were… what did he say? Sweet on me. *Doce por mim.* That is how we say it in English."

He kissed the tip of her nose and said, "That is true. I like the taste of you." Enjoying his interpretation of the phrase, she kissed him back.

What followed in the next weeks, as had been the case when Andy visited the first time, was extensive conversation about where the guests would stay and where to take them, although Adrienne was sure they were already making plans of their own. Lourenço felt Adrienne should stay with him, letting Andy and his children have the two apartments. She was not so sure.

"I don't know. It feels too soon. Won't people talk?"

"They might, but it shouldn't be so important." It was, however, he knew. People may be happy for them, but they lived in a village. A traditional one.

"How about Andy and the kids staying here? This is a big house. There is plenty of room."

"It would be too much," said Adrienne. "An imposition. And too much work."

"*Não,* not so much."

The argument went on, ending with a grudging agreement by Adrienne that the visitors would not be in Veredas long, a week maybe. They would be traveling around the country most of the rest of the time. It was decided. Kathryn would take the small apartment with her in town while Andy and Jake would stay with Lourenço.

She wrote to Andy to share this idea and ask for more details about where he hoped to take the kids while they were here. And whether he wanted her to make any arrangements for transportation or places to stay. His letter back let her know he would be renting a car and had made some reservations already, leaving time for Veredas and a visit to Porto. He invited her to meet them in Lisbon and join in the fun, saying

Lourenço would be welcome, too. This written with a smiley-face following the sentence.

Adrienne spent the end of the month finishing projects underway, cleaning and stocking the two apartments, and helping Lourenço at the house. Having looked at the proposed itinerary, he had decided not to go with her to Lisbon or on the coastal drive north where Jake would be able to surf and the others to lounge on the beach. He wanted them to have time together. He would go along on the trip to Porto and had told Ana and Fernao about the plans.

With the focus on the coming visit, Adrienne and Lourenço seemed to forget any discomfort they had felt about their relationship being noticeable. They went about their daily routines and preparations, sharing most nights together. At her apartment. When he asked her to stay one night after dinner at the house, she looked at him carefully.

"*Por favor,*" he said. "I want you to feel comfortable."

"Are you comfortable with me being here? I mean, with us being here."

"Jacolin's ghost is not here. Not lurking about watching us. And even if it were, it would not be an angry ghost, but a friendly one."

Their lovemaking that night was intense, focused. As if each were conscious of a change, another step taken. Adrienne lay back and catching her breath, said "Who would have thought?"

"Thought what?"

"That lovemaking could be so... so wonderful."

"Adrienne, was it not so for you and Arthur?"

"No, not so much. It wasn't bad. Arthur just was not so interested. Didn't seem to take too much pleasure in it. Like it was something he thought he should do. So, we did. Not all that often, and it was perfunctory. What's the word? *Superficial*? Not so inventive." Adrienne giggled.

Lourenço rolled back to her and began to run his hands over her body. Slowly, slowly. Searching, reaching, finding. "Let me show you inventive."

Ana and Fernao arrived unexpectedly the next morning. "It was a last-minute decision." Ana was already talking as she let herself in through the kitchen door. "School let out and Fernao has been working hard to meet an important deadline, so can take some time off. We're having a long weekend on the coast and thought... we'd stop on our way... ". Her voice trailed off as she realized Adrienne was sitting with Lourenço eating breakfast at the kitchen table.

Lourenço gave her a small smile and said, "*Café?* There is some on the stove. I'll go help Fernao."

Ana stared at him wordlessly as he walked past her, then at Adrienne. The silence continued as she poured herself coffee and sank into a chair at the table. Adrienne began to worry. *Was Ana's earlier happiness for them in jeopardy with the reality of an actual relationship?* But her anxiety disappeared as Ana began to smile, then to stifle something more resembling a smirk.

"I don't know what I should say. *Parabéns?* Congratulations! *Que maravilhoso?* How wonderful! Or just *obrigada*?" Now she was beaming, her eyes dancing.

Adrienne's response was cut short by the children rushing in with excited talk about the flowers in the garden and would their mother please come out to see the birds nest in the tree by the driveway. Fernao followed and came over to give her a hug with his "*Bom Dia*".

As Inês tugged her by the hand, Ana leaned over and whispered in Adrienne's ear, "I want to hear about this." The smile on her face and on Fernao's stilled any fears they were displeased with the turn of events.

Chapter 18: *The Fun of Travel*

As the train pulled into Lisbon, Adrienne searched out the window for Andy, Kathyrn and Jake. They had arrived late the night before and should have breakfasted already and worked out the jetlag accompanying the long flight.

There he was, scrutinizing at each train car as it passed him on the platform. She lined up to disembark and waved. "Andy, here I am."

With a good long hug, Andy said, "I couldn't rouse the kids. Sleepyheads. But they should be up by the time we get back to the hotel. It's the same one we stayed in last time. Not far."

Adrienne was somewhat relieved, knowing she could talk openly with Andy about Lourenço and how their relationship had changed. He was, as she thought he would be, unsurprised.

"I told you, didn't I. He was already half in love with you when I was here at Christmas."

She stopped and pivoted to look at him. "Whoa. Love? That might not be true. I don't... well, I'm not sure... I... "

"Okay, okay. Maybe it is too soon to say it, but maybe not. He seems to be a pretty confident guy. Like when he makes up his mind, he makes up his mind." He cocked his head at her, "Oh, I guess it's you that's not sure."

She gave him a shrug and sighed, "It's true. I worry." As they walked, she told him how she had struggled with the idea of relinquishing her newfound freedom and about the fear she had voiced that first night about having to leave Veredas if things did not work out.

He was sympathetic, but shook his head and said, "Maybe that's part of it. The new freedom. Having choices to make."

She went silent and it hit her—*I hadn't thought of it like that. But yes, I suppose it's true.* She stayed quiet until at the door of the hotel she reached out to slow him with a hand on his arm, "You're a pretty smart guy, Andy."

As they hoped, Kathryn and Jake were in the lobby, sipping coffee. It was a joyful reunion with hugs all around as Adrienne got checked in. They left immediately to begin their tour of Lisbon. They visited some of the same places she and Andy had seen before, but there also were new sites, more art and history. They tramped through the old neighborhoods and up steep cobblestoned streets, dodging more tourists than Adrienne and Andy had encountered during their winter trip. On the second day, they went to the Museum of Contemporary Art, and as they knew she would be, Kathryn was enthralled and remained to explore more thoroughly while Jake made his way to the University of Lisbon to see the campus. Adrienne and Andy wandered the streets near the market where the other two would join them for dinner.

On the final day, with them all agreeing there was far too much to see, they went across the bridge to the monument, *Cristo Rei.* It had been cold when Andy and Adrienne had visited in January so the chance to stand in the summer sun to view the city across the Tagus was a welcome change. They walked along the docks on the south side of the river and took a ferry across, wandering back to the hotel before a last dinner and another chance to hear *Fado* while trying *ginjinha,* a liqueur made from sour cherries and served in shot glasses and edible chocolate cups. A specialty in Lisbon.

≈≈≈≈≈≈≈

Ericeira was a short drive away, with several famous beaches, the first of three stops on the drive north. Their rooms were basic but with good views, easy access to the beach, and surfboard rentals onsite for Jake. A routine was quickly established—early breakfasts and off to surf or walk or sit in the sun. They would check out after lunch and take a short drive to another beach up the coast.

Peniche, the second town, was on a peninsula with the ocean on three sides. Because of its popularity, it felt more touristy, crowded, but they found a few historic sites among the bars and shops. They ate dinner at the beach, sampling a spicy *frango assado,* well-known as Piri Piri chicken, marinated and grilled on the restaurant terrace. This was followed by Nazaré, suggested by Leonor and Ana and Fernao. It was their favorite. A smaller fishing village with a more traditional feel despite the tourists. Older men and women walked the boardwalk and sat on benches in the town square—a few of the women in colorful headscarves and traditional embroidered aprons over multilayered petticoats.

Then it was on to Veredas. On the way were two stops to marvel at sights of particular note—neither of which Adrienne had seen. The ancient gothic Monastery of Batalha, built in the late 1300s with striking stained-glass windows and intricate pinnacles. The shrine at Fátima where they had to push their way through groups of religious pilgrims, celebrating the apparitions of the Virgin Mary reportedly witnessed by three children in 1917.

Kathryn and Jake had known her mostly as part of Arthur and Adrienne, their uncle and aunt, and had been none too close. So, learning she had simply landed in Veredas and stayed, alone and without a real plan, was a revelation. In the car, as they neared the village, they plied her with questions—why there, why she had stayed, and why she had decided to sell her house and move back. Adrienne answered as honestly as she could, but in the end, the best response she could come up with was a shrug and, "I guess I just found myself here".

Lourenço stepped out of his workshop when they parked by the apartment. "*Olá,* Lourenço!" called Andy, who motioned Kathryn and Jake over to meet him. Adrienne slid under his arm and gave him a light kiss, much to the surprise of the two young people. Without hesitation, he kissed her soundly and kept his arm around her shoulders as he was introduced. He left with Andy and Jake and when Kathryn was settled, Adrienne walked her through town to the house for dinner. They stopped often to introduce her to people, but for the first time, Kathryn had Adrienne to herself and could ask about her new life and her new relationship.

"Aunt Adrienne."

"How about we switch to just Adrienne? Doesn't make me feel so dowdy. Like I should be wearing an apron and making cookies or something."

"OK, Adrienne. How did you decide this was the place to stay? I mean, it is pretty small and not much different from other towns we saw on the way here. And why Portugal? I don't even know that."

So, Adrienne gave her more detail about coming to Portugal on vacation and how dreary the tour was, the bus trip to Veredas, and getting off without thinking. The first anxious night in the village and the following few weeks of relaxed discovery.

"I have to admit, I just fell into it. Into Veredas, anyway." She lifted her arms to encompass the village around her. "It wasn't planned, it just happened. It was one day, followed by another, and another. Until I seemed to fit in. It kinda grew on me. I liked the people. I liked the feel of the town and the countryside around it."

"Pretty big change from New Brunswick."

"You can say that three times. It was part of its appeal. At least in the beginning. Now, to tell you the truth, I hardly think of New Jersey at all. And certainly not as home. Other than you kids and your dad, and your grandmother, I can't say I miss anything about it. Well, maybe the easy access to a bigger city with museums and shops and stuff, but even that I don't miss much."

"And how about Lourenço? Is he a part of the draw here?" Kathryn looked out the corner of her eye at Adrienne, not sure what her reaction to the question would be. She saw a smile and a shake of the head.

"No, he wasn't at all a part of the picture when I first came. I mean, he did rent me the apartment, but he was kind of cold and grouchy, not at all welcoming." She thought for a minute before going on, "I thought of him when I was in New Jersey selling the house. Wondering what he would think when I came back. But even then, it wasn't something that factored into my decision. At least not consciously," she laughed and added, "Another thing I seem to have fallen into. I'm still not sure about it, but for the moment I am happy to let things unfold."

They were nearing the house and Kathryn said, "I'm sure there is more to the story. I'd like to hear it sometime."

"Maybe. And maybe you should ask Lourenço. His perspective might be interesting."

≈≈≈≈≈≈≈

Their days in Veredas were a round of visits and introductions to friends, hikes on the trails above the village, and evenings at Lourenço's with fine food and good wine. On their last afternoon, Kathryn went to Leonor's to watch the candle-making process. She had hit it off with Carolina and enjoyed the chance to talk with someone nearer her own age about living in a small town. Andy rode off with Aldo and Tomás on a bike trip, returning with renewed enthusiasm for making Veredas into a jumping-off point and glad Jake had joined them as the three younger men had bonded immediately.

"Veredas is perfect for it. And since I was here at Christmas things have popped up that will help. Aldo took us by Benita's guesthouse. It was full! And the new ice cream counter and the bar now selling pizza. He said there will be a new shop opening soon with bike gear and stuff for hiking. He told me how you helped with the marketing materials. You did a great job getting things moving."

"That wasn't really my doing. People were ready to grow. But it's nice they think I had a hand in it. Makes me feel a part of things here."

Dinner that night included Leonor, Nicholau and his wife Ileana, and Doroteia and Rehor, all of whom brought a favorite dish to make sure Kathryn and Jake had a good sample of the home cooking of Portugal. It felt like a celebration and a coming together of families.

They left the next morning in two cars as Lourenço and Adrienne would be driving back to Veredas after the stay in Porto while the others would head back to Lisbon for the trip home. It gave the two of them a chance to talk alone, a rare occurrence over the last few days.

"I think the kids… I should stop calling them kids, Kathryn is twenty and Jake almost eighteen… anyway, they seem to be enjoying themselves. And interested in what they're seeing."

Lourenço responded with a nod and a chuckle, "And it looks as if they've gotten used to the idea you are happy here. Have a different life. Both Kathryn and Jake asked me about the two of us."

"What did you say?"

He reached over and took her hand, "That I thought you were ready to be happy. And I was ready to be happy, too. And maybe it was as simple as that."

"Maybe it is," she said and was quiet as she turned the idea over in her mind. *Maybe it is.*

They spent the afternoon at the Casa Ferreirinha winery in the Douro Valley, tasting the *vinho verde,* green or young wine popular in the north of Portugal, *Barca Velha,* a red table wine much-loved throughout the country, and of course, the famous port. The winding roads to Porto afterward were driven with care, followed by several wrong turns in the city before they found the hotel. Lourenço was staying with Ana and Fernao, so left the others there with directions to the restaurant where they would meet later.

Over dinner, Ana excitedly shared that the *Museu Serralves* had officially opened earlier in the month. She was sure Kathryn would want to spend time there and the others would enjoy the museum and could walk in the park if they tired of being indoors. She planned to join them as she was on vacation from her part-time teaching job.

While Andy and Fernao caught up on the computer world, Jake was able to learn more about the university where Ana taught, the *Universidade Portucalense*. He had read about it and wondered what they meant by an international education since the offerings he had seen covered psychology and science as well as law, economics, and culture. Seemed an interesting mix to him.

"It is an inter-disciplinary approach to education," Ana said. "With visiting professors from across Europe and other countries. So, many perspectives. And partnerships with companies as well, where students work on projects. It is how I came to know about the program. Fernao's company is part of the technology network. Mostly new enterprises."

"And growing," chimed in Fernao. "When we started with the university a few years ago, the group was small. Now there are eight companies from all over Europe. I think it is important for students to work in the fields they are interested in while they study. Helps them decide what they want to do."

"Although they talk about it at Temple," said Kathryn, "they don't have many opportunities for work connected to art degrees. Some internships for people in art education and in conservation, but not much else. The best of the professors bring in speakers who are working artists, having them talk about what their lives are like."

As the conversation drifted between education and technology and art, Lourenço leaned back and observed, pleased to see the easy exchange of ideas and what could be the growing connection between his family and Adrienne's. As he drove home with Ana and Fernao they both expressed the same thing, and the hope Adrienne's family shared the feeling.

The remainder of the visit bore this out, with a clear friendship developing between Ana and Kathryn and between Fernao and Andy and Jake. There was time at Serralves and its park, a walk through the historic downtown to view the art deco buildings and ever-present *azulejo* ceramic tiles, and along the river to see the flat-bottomed boats delivering wine from the vineyards. A trip to Matosinhos Beach allowed the children to play on the shore and Jake to observe the local surfing. Of equal interest for him was the *Universidade Portucalense,* where they stopped to see the main campus and he went with Ana to the administration office to pick up an information packet on admission.

"Who knows," Adrienne said as she and Lourenço returned to Veredas, "maybe Jake will end up in Portugal, too. He was pretty interested in seeing the universities in Lisbon and Porto."

"As we said, you started a trend. He does seem like he is searching for a place to explore."

"Makes me feel less sad about their leaving. The trip seemed so short."

He took her hand and gave it a squeeze. "I don't doubt Andy will be back. He and Fernao seemed to be planning something. I don't know exactly what. And maybe Jake. The fact that there is good surfing here doesn't hurt."

Chapter 19: *Summer Days*

Adrienne settled into the routine of warm sunny days with walks in the hills, visits with friends, a little work when it came her way, and evenings on her terrace or Lourenço's. Their relationship had become an easy one, without much question about where it was going or whether it was going anywhere. There were smiles and nods of greeting on the street, at the Saturday market, and events in the *praça*. There were no raised eyebrows or sideways glances as one or the other would be seen walking home in the morning, at least none either noticed.

Near the end of July, they celebrated Lourenço's birthday. A small party at the house, catered by Nicholau, who made Lourenço's favorite dish, *caracóis,* tiny snails in broth. As Adrienne passed around the accompanying basket of fresh bread she felt as much the hostess as Lourenço the host. In August, news of yet another celebration spread throughout Veredas. Marissa and Marcos were to be married. The women smiled when they heard and said it was about time. The men crossed their arms over their chests when they saw him and said he had better treat her right. The little girls sighed. The boys teased them both. Lourenço looked at Adrienne and wondered.

The church was filled with family and friends, many of the town's residents, and a few stray tourists who lingered at the door to observe the service. Marcos's best man, *padrinho,* was his oldest brother who had traveled from the east with his father, mother, and four other siblings. They were all welcomed by Marissa's family and treated as long-lost relatives by Adao and Rafaela, the bakery owners. Marissa's maid of honor, the *madrinha,* was Valera, Leonor's daughter, who had chided her about waiting so long to marry but now with a smile saying it had been the right decision.

The reception after the service was held in the adjacent school, the largest space available in the village. It was catered, of course, by Nicholau. There were *bacalhau* and *chouriço,* and cold meats served on wooden planks, as well as a variety of cheeses accompanied by plums, peaches, figs and grapes. The dessert table overflowed with pastries from the bakery and the wedding cake, a traditional one with a covering of almond marzipan and egg custard filling. On a long table at the back, small gifts had been left, most for the apartment where the couple would live, but an urn was filled with money to help pay for the honeymoon, a trip to the east and Marcos' village to celebrate with the community where he grew up.

The reception flowed out to the town square along with the wines served with dinner—red and white, sparkling brut, and port. They had all been provided as a wedding gift by the Oliveiras, who employed Marissa's father at the winery. Couples danced in the square until 2 a.m. Lourenço and Adrienne among them.

They wandered back to Lourenço's hand in hand, humming along with the music they could still hear from the *praça.*

"It was a lovely celebration. Nicholau outdid himself with the food. And I think Marcos' family felt so welcomed. Adao said they were a little shy and overwhelmed by all the activity this week, but they were certainly sociable at the reception."

"Hmmm," murmured Lourenço, not paying close attention.

"Lourenço?"

He shook himself and looked over. "Sorry. I was thinking. About the wedding. About Marissa and Marcos. They have so much ahead of them." His voice trailed off, then he added, "And about us." He went quiet again and Adrienne waited.

"I know we are much older. But I think we, too, could have much ahead of us. Could share that time." Now, he waited.

Adrienne wasn't surprised by his statement, but in a way had dreaded it. It meant she would have to confront the dilemma churning in the back of her mind the past few months. *Do I take this next step with Lourenço even though it feels like abandoning the new, independent path I thought I was taking?* It had been nagging at her from the start. She thought back to their first night together and Lourenço's reassurances.

"You know what I have been worried about. What I said on that first night. Talked about coming home from Porto." She turned to face him. "I do not regret one second of the time we've spent together. I don't want you to think my hesitation now is dissatisfaction or unhappiness with our being together. I hope, as you said, we have more to share. I have thought a lot about what you said to Kathryn, that we both were simply ready to be happy… that I was ready to be happy. Andy said something that made me think, too. That the freedom I was experiencing meant having choices to make. I hadn't considered that."

She stood on her toes stretching up to kiss him. "I want to believe I can choose to be with you and also enjoy this newfound freedom. That both can happen at the same time. I am not sure it is true, but I want to believe it." She kissed him again before going on, "Can you give me a little more time to sort this out? To wrestle with my uncertainty?"

Lourenço raised her hand to his lips and brushed it with a soft kiss. "*Claro, querida.*"

Over coffee the next day, Adrienne confided in Leonor and Doroteia, explaining how she had struggled with the decision to begin a relationship with Lourenço and why. How she had worried about having to leave Veredas if things did not work out. How she worried still about reverting to the tentative colorless person she had been when she first came to Portugal. And how she hoped to move ahead in her life.

"*Tu? Não, não,*" Doroteia shook her head vehemently. "I remember the woman who crept into my store. Shy, unsure. But she left with a beautiful *Barcelos* vase and big red chair. That woman knew what she wanted, just as you do now!"

"I remember her, too," said Leonor. "Coming in for a much-needed haircut and walking out ten years younger. She is sitting here with us today, a changed, happier woman."

Adrienne's eyes teared up at both the kind recollections and the fervent assurances she was strong and could choose a path for herself. She reached out to take the hands of her friends and received hugs in return.

Chapter 20: *Moving In*

Adrienne moved to Lourenço's at the end of September. A momentous decision on her part, one agonized over for the entire month. She would spend a night at the house feeling comforted and certain of the future, then a night alone at her apartment, up in the wee hours on the terrace struggling with the pros and cons. Finally, she told herself, *Enough! If it doesn't work out, I'll come back.*

The move itself was easy. One carload. As she unpacked her clothes in the bedroom closet, she felt a loosening of her shoulders and neck, but it was making a workspace in the second-floor room Lourenço had cleared for her that gave her a truer sense of belonging. *My space,* she thought as she set out her computer, stored supplies in the desk, and stacked her books on a side table.

Adrienne became familiar with the house. At first it was just a perusal, coming to know where things were, what was in that closet or that set of drawers. Slowly, she inserted herself into each room. Turning a chair in the living room to face the morning sun where she sat with coffee. Changing a lamp in the living room to give her better light. Moving the desk in her small office so she could look at the hillside and the terraced fields. Asking Lourenço about shifting something in the kitchen to make it more accessible. She was aware of how he watched these changes—watched with a small, satisfied smile, as he, too, felt the settling in and saluted it.

More important, more powerful for Adrienne was the realization as they sat with a glass of wine on the screened porch—the garden was calling to her.

"Lourenço, I know the garden was a special place for Jacolin. I wonder if it will be okay for me to work with it or whether that would be painful for you… to see me there."

He looked out at the garden and said, "I have thought about it, knowing your love of gardening. How you talked about the one you created in America. I hoped the garden would be one of the things to help you make the decision to move here. I have pictured you there. I think Jacolin would be happy to know someone would give it the love she did."

Initially done with some caution—a snip here and a weeding there—work in the garden soon became a part of Adrienne's routine, taken on with increasing confidence and enjoyment of the feel of good rich soil and its distinctive smell. With the changing fall weather, it focused to some degree on preparation for the colder months ahead—cleaning the flower beds of spent blossoms and fallen leaves, cutting back perennials, tilling what had been the vegetable plot, and spreading mulch from the pile of decaying matter Lourenço had created when he had come back home. Then she turned to decisions about removing overgrown shrubs and relocating plants no longer thriving.

One afternoon Adrienne sat with the sun warming her face and let it relax her. Over the past year, she had seen the garden in each season and had some remembrance of where the early spring blooms first appeared and the places with the lushest summer flowerings. She let those images wash over her. There was not much to change. Jacolin had had taste. Or had it been Lourenço's mother? She conjured up memories of her garden in New Jersey, what she had especially loved. The shape of a favorite tree. The spacing between the garden beds and grassy areas. The look of particular flowers. When she opened her eyes again, she had a fresh perspective. How to make the garden her own.

With a trip to Aveiro and some happily shared transplants from Leonor, new bulbs and plants found homes alongside the house and in the beds throughout the yard. Adrienne had ideas for more additions but wanted to wait and see how the changes she had made worked out. This did not dissuade her from sketching plans for spring vegetable planting and summer annuals.

With a turn in the weather, her efforts shifted to a neglected backyard shed where garden tools and unused pots crowded the shelves. Adrienne spent two days sorting through what was there and filling Lourenço's truck with things for Doroteia's shop she knew she would not use and unredeemable items to be discarded. With Lourenço's help, shelves were repaired, tool hangers installed, and a sturdier potting table set under newly washed windows.

"It has new life," he said as they admired the clean and now more brightly-lit space and the tidy garden beyond. "Jacolin would approve."

"I almost felt her here with me while I was working. Like she was looking over my shoulder and giving me advice."

"She definitely had opinions and did not hesitate to share them. Especially about the garden. She and Leonor would have long discussions about new things to try and she would read up on how best to cultivate them."

"I've seen the books in the library but haven't had time to examine them. And I have to admit I haven't made it much further with the book you gave me. My Portuguese is not as good as I thought. It's slow going with the dictionary."

"Maybe we should get you a translation. You could read them side-by-side."

More important to Adrienne, however, were the gardening books. She spent an afternoon pulling out and perusing each one. She ended up with a small stack she took back to her chair in the living room. What interested her most were the handwritten notes alongside many of the plant descriptions—Jacolin's notes—some identifying successes and others the failures and attempts to transplant to better locations. Some simply exclaimed her happiness at the performance of a favorite. She was smiling and nodding about one when Lourenço came in, sat across from her, and asked what was so amusing.

She was about to say that he had found two women of like minds and similar tastes, but instead said, "I am just agreeing with Jacolin's assessment of what works well in the garden. How the plants in the front should not be too large or they obstruct the view. And how the plants in the back need to be protected from the northeasterly winds.'

As if he had read her mind, Lourenço said, "You two would have worked well together." He sat back and turned to gaze out the window.

"Lourenço? Are you alright?"

"*Sim,* just remembering. How much Jacolin loved the time she put into the garden and what came of it. In a way, it makes me sad that the two of you could not meet. But that is difficult, too. A bit confusing… balancing these thoughts in my head."

"Yes," she whispered. "It must be. I am sorry if I have moved too fast, or stepped where I should not have."

Lourenço shook himself and looked back to her. "*Não,* there will be times when the memories are strong, but that is not a bad thing. I am happy you are here. I would not have it any other way."

≈≈≈≈≈≈≈

Re-shelving the books gave Adrienne the idea of perusing the library more carefully. After her daily walks, maybe a visit, and the English tutoring sessions which had remained popular, she retreated to the library. At first, she had browsed, but in pulling a book or two of interest off the shelf realized many were dusty and cobwebbed. She decided a more systematic approach was in order so she could clean as she went.

On one of the lower shelves were children's books, most appearing to be Ana's, but a few were more recent purchases, likely for the grandchildren's visits. Another easily accessible shelf held well-thumbed carpentry, construction, and machine repair books, clearly well used. Higher in the bookcase were literature and poetry. Next to Jacolin's gardening books were hardcover art volumes that must have been hers as well and older ones on needlework and sewing that could have belonged to Lourenço's mother.

When she climbed the library ladder to reach the highest shelf, filled primarily with thick tomes of what appeared to be reference volumes and an old encyclopedia set, she also found a large section on Portuguese history, World War II, and the Spanish Civil War. Most of the books were quite dated, but Adrienne wished her Portuguese were better. She would have liked to read more about the country's history. As she reached the top rung of the ladder, she saw a stack of large scrapbooks lying flat on the shelf. All but one had well-worn black leather covers. She carefully pulled down each one and carried them to the dining room table where there was more light.

She was preparing to take a look when she heard Lourenço come in the kitchen door, back from the shop where he had spent the day with Aldo and Tomás. As she helped him unpack a bag of groceries, she told him about her find.

"I haven't looked at them yet. There are five."

"*Sim*, there is at least one my grandmother put together and my mother did some, too. Photographs and keepsakes, I remember. I haven't looked at them in a long time."

He seemed a little reluctant and poured them each a glass of wine before they sat at the long table. He took the album from the top of the stack, the newest looking one, and opened it. On the first page was a formal wedding photograph—Jacolin and Lourenço and their families.

"Oh," Adrienne stared at it, turned to him and said, "I'm sorry. I should've realized there would be pictures of her. Of the two of you."

"*Não*, it's okay. These were happy times."

They leafed through the pages one by one. Mostly candid shots, some in the garden or the house, others walking in the terraced hills above the village. There was one photograph of a pregnant Jacolin, followed by another of her holding a small bundle.

"Ana's first day home," he said. There were many more of Ana's growing up with pictures from school and with friends and some from vacations in the mountains and at the beach. These were followed by photographs of Ana and Fernao, their wedding, and a few with Joao as a baby, a toddler. Then nothing. Just blank pages.

"After Jacolin died, I quit taking pictures. Well, not entirely. I have some of Inês and Gabriela and of the whole family when they have come to visit at Christmas. But I never got around to putting them in the album."

Adrienne put her hand on his shoulder and let him sit with his thoughts. He sighed "Maybe it's time to do it. And give the album to Ana. I think she might like it."

Lourenço closed the album and set it aside, opening another from the stack, the cover slightly mottled. "*Ai,* from *minha avó,* my grandmother."

The pages showed faded studio photographs. A seated man or woman and a couple with the man resting his hand on the back of her chair. Some were dated, others not. Lourenço was able to identify who was who, moving through the years of great-grandparents and grandparents. In the latter part of the album, the photographs were interspersed with postcards, some sepias and some hand-colored—castles, cathedrals, hillsides, a coastal village, Porto above the Douro River. And occasionally, a pressed flower, a rose, with a date on the page.

"It was my grandparents' anniversary, I think. Can't quite remember without looking it up."

"I wonder whether that rose is still in the garden," said Adrienne. "Probably not, it's quite a while ago. But some wild roses live a very long time and there are a couple of well-established climbing roses along the back fence."

The next album was similar—older posed photographs, wedding shots, and more candid ones. "This is my mother's family," Lourenço said as he flipped through the pages, most of which showed a young girl growing up. "*Minha mãe,* my mother. You can tell she was doted on. The only child."

The last photograph was of a wedding couple. Lourenço's fingers lingered over it. "My mother and father." He set the album aside, stretched and said, "How about we save the last two for after dinner. We've been at this a while." He seemed hesitant.

"Do you want to stop? Is it too much? All this reminiscence? We can save these last ones for another time." asked Adrienne.

"*Não, não*. I'm just hungry."

They talked of other things over dinner. Andy's letter saying Jake had applied to two colleges—the *Universidade de Lisboa's* to study history and the *Universidade Portucalense* in Porto. Adrienne plans to help Leonor with some deliveries, a chance for a day trip to Aveiro and Coimbra. Lourenço's project at the Oliveiras' winery to patch the garage roof before colder weather set in. It was easy, idle conversation, but the albums at the other end of the table seemed to lie in wait.

Finishing with clean up and the dishes, they brought the last of their wine back to the dining room and resumed the exploration. Lourenço pulled the next album to him. It began with a few photographs of Lourenço's grandparents, including one of his grandmother holding two infants. "My father and my uncle Silvio," he said.

Adrienne drew back to look at him. "Lourenço, you've never talked about an uncle."

"They were twins. But I didn't know him. Not at all. He left before I was born. A disagreement with my grandfather, about what was happening in Spain and what side Portugal should support in its Civil War. He went to fight against the Nationalists, against Franco. He came back once but soon left again. My father told me he had tried to find Silvio after the war, but never did. It was another thing he didn't want to talk about. Another thing that brought on his sadness."

They paged through the album, watching his father and uncle become young men. Shots from the house, the village, and hiking in the hills and rockier mountains. At the end was another photograph of his parents' wedding and then a blank page where something had been removed.

"I wonder what it was," said Adrienne.

"You'll see," said Lourenço, opening the last album. The first page was labeled *Lourenço* in big letters, with the date of his birth underneath. Then, two photographs. One of Lourenço's father leaning over a bed holding his mother and an infant. The other of a young man in the armchair Adrienne recognized from the living room, carefully holding a blanketed bundle.

"That's me in the blanket. And my uncle holding me. The photo was taken on his last visit. I think he came home to see me. I guess my grandfather took it out of my grandmother's album. But he didn't destroy it. He must have laid it aside somewhere and my mother found it. Put it in this one, knowing my father would treasure it." Lourenço gazed at the photograph for another moment, then said, "OK, now you'll see what a funny boy I was. No laughing!"

But they did laugh, moving from one page to the next—Lourenço running on the beach, astride a rocking horse, in a cape with a sword, at school with other children, and a serious-looking one at his confirmation. And many with Rehor, at the house, swimming, hiking in the mountains.

"I recognize him," said Adrienne. "You could mistake him for Rehe."

"*Sim,* the same look as a boy."

The last pages of the album were of a slightly older Lourenço with friends, young men with their arms around one another's shoulders. And a few with young women. Then one, with Jacolin. Both of them looking somewhat shy.

Chapter 21: *Christmas, Again, and New*

The days sped by for both of them with preparations for the holiday visit from Ana, Fernao and the children. Lourenço hoped to make Adrienne's first Christmas at the house memorable so was in a happy whirl of stocking up on provisions and decorating. He unearthed colorful lights from the attic to string around the house and entryway. He carried in seasoned oak logs from the woodpile for the fireplace. He got out the creche figures for underneath the Christmas tree but did not build the manger, wanting to wait for the children's arrival to do so.

Adrienne went from room to room distributing candles in freshly shined holders and filling vases with holly, *azevinho,* she had cut from the garden. She spent an afternoon with Doroteia and her children baking cookies and *Bolo Rei,* one of which she brought home. She pulled out cookbooks the two of them poured over after dinner to figure out the meals they would make.

Together they joined the Oliveiras to cut Christmas trees above the winery. The sun was bright as they walked from the cars into the forested area and Valerie Oliveira took Adrienne's arm. They had met just once before, at Lourenço's party the previous year. The conversation started slowly, a little formally, but warmed quickly.

"I am not as young as I once was, not out walking the land like I used to, but I couldn't pass up this beautiful day," she said. "And thank you for joining us this year. It is a tradition

Lourenço and his family participated in every year. I am happy you can be a part of it. Lourenço said it was special, your first Christmas at the house."

"Valerie, it is you I should thank for including me. Lourenço was quite excited, telling me of times he and his father had cut trees with your family, and later he and Jacolin."

"*Por favor,* please call me Vivi. Everyone does. It is an *apelida,* what is that in English?"

"Nickname."

"*Sim,* that's right. It is something of a joke. It is related to olives. We are the Oliveira family. And, we grow olives as well as grapes for the wine, as does my own family. So... Vivi," she gave a wave of her hand and laughed.

They spent the rest of the walk getting to know each other, Vivi talking about growing up not too far away and her life at the winery, Adrienne about her move to Veredas. Vivi was curious about the decision.

"It is a little hard for me to understand. Someone like me, living so closely with my family and then here. So tied to the land." She looked shyly at Adrienne before asking, "It was not this way for you, growing up?"

"*Não,*" Adrienne answered. "No, sadly not. It is certainly true for many families in America, to be wholly connected to a place. To each other. But not mine. We moved more than once when I was a child. When I married, my husband and I had a house not terribly close to my family. I suppose that made it easier for me to leave. To come to Veredas."

"And now that you are here, does it feel different?"

"Ai, sim." Adrienne nodded and her face lit up. "It is like I tried to explain to my niece and nephew when they were visiting last summer. I had to make a decision. Once I did, it felt right. Like I was meant to be here. Like I fit in, even though I am not Portuguese, even though I am not a girl from the country, or from a small town like Veredas."

Vivi smiled, "I am glad it is so. We are different, you and me. But finding yourself is important. *Sim*?"

"Yes, *absolutamente*."

They had fallen behind the others but catching up they found the men selecting trees to consider, waiting for their opinions. When the cutting was finished, they loaded the cars and shared cups of the winery's port before heading back.

As they drove home, Lourenço asked how she had gotten on with Vivi. "She was always a little separate from the village, busy at the winery and at the hotel."

"I think she's a little shy. I got the impression she has lived most of her life within the confines of the family and the family's business. She says she may be slowing down, but it is still her life."

"I'm sure that's true."

They unloaded the tree and set it up in the living room, Adrienne sitting down to admire it, jumping up to move it slightly so the best side faced the room. Lourenço brought in two glasses and a bottle of the Oliveiras' port, pouring for her then himself.

"A fine tree. Just the right size for the room. We can go to the attic tomorrow for the decorations. There are several boxes."

Adrienne had been to the attic and remembered the jumble of boxes, the old chests tucked under the eaves, and a small divan. She had thought at the time what a perfect spot for children to hide themselves away and wondered whether Lourenço had done so. He had said not, that while it was not off-limits, his father had made it clear it was his private place. Somehow the missive had stuck and Lourenço had said he rarely went up there.

He repeated this as they moved boxes to the stairwell, wiping one off and coughing at the plume of dust that arose. "I only come up on occasions like this week. To get the Christmas lights and now the tree ornaments. Probably should clean it sometime."

"I can help. I'm curious about what's in the chests. They look pretty old."

"I know Jacolin came up to explore. After my father and mother died. She must have gone through all the boxes and chests to see what was there. It's where the photo albums came from. She brought them down and put them in the library. Along with some silver pieces and cutlery that are in the dining room. I remember her saying there were old linens and blankets, clothes, papers, and other things that didn't seem to have much value. I think she meant to go back and sort them out but never did. At least not that I know of. Got busy with other things, I guess."

"Well, maybe after Christmas, when we take down the decorations."

They spent the afternoon decorating the tree. Lovely old ornaments— roosters of *Barcelos,* angels, stars, hand-painted balls, and small ceramic pieces of *azulejo*. There also were many wooden ones. Lourenço pointed out those he had made and those of his father and grandfather. He put the large star alongside the creche figures. The children would help place it atop the tree.

It was dark now. Adrienne lit candles as Lourenço made a fire. They sat back to admire their work.

"No lights," he said. "I know the children like them, but we never had them when I was a child. So, I keep to the tradition. It looks almost exactly as it did then."

"It's beautiful." Adrienne thought back on her own childhood Christmases. There had been some early ones where the magic seemed alive. Later the holidays were fraught, with a focus on shopping, who got what and how many, and rather formal Christmas parties. There was nothing much to reminisce about after her father left. Her mother could not mount the interest to organize much of a celebration.

"You look thoughtful." Lourenço reaching for her hand.

"I was remembering what Christmas was like when I was little," she said, and described the best parts. The fun of decorating the tree while her father sang carols and they drank cocoa. Driving the neighborhoods to see the lights people had put up. The half-eaten cookie and half-full glass of milk on the table near the tree. Her father making a special breakfast after opening presents, about the only time he did so. She did not talk about how it had changed or the first sweet Christmases with Arthur when she had tried to recreate the joy of her childhood, or how that, too, had slipped away over time.

But the Christmas that unfolded in her new home dispelled any wistful, lingering memories for Adrienne. Joao, Inês and Gabriela were ecstatic to see the tree, the youngest especially as Lourenço held her up to place the star on top. Everyone took part in creating the nativity scene. Ana and Fernao were relaxed, completely at ease with Adrienne's new role in Lourenço's life.

There was no big party this year, just visits back and forth with friends, short walks on the cool afternoons, a quiet Christmas Eve *Consoada* and midnight mass. Andy called them on Christmas Day and they passed the telephone from hand-to-hand to wish him *Feliz Natal*. It was as picture-perfect as she could ever have imagined.

Chapter 22: *Discovery*

They were as good as their word, taking on the attic clean-up when they packed away the Christmas decorations. It was a messy job with years of accumulated dust and cobwebs. The boxes were sorted and Lourenço carted off several holding flower vases and dishes neither wanted, toys broken beyond repair, worn boots and shoes, and much-mended clothes. While he was loading his truck, Adrienne inched out one of the two chests from under the eaves and opened it. As Jacolin had said, old linens, monogrammed pillowcases and sheets with lace edging, some quite pretty she thought as she ran her hands over the smooth fabric. An embroidered blanket and a quilt made of now-shredding silk. There also were faded vintage dresses from what must have been the early 1900s, including a wedding dress of sleek satin and small pearls. Tucked in amongst them were odds and ends—playing cards, a porcelain doll head, a small box of shells and rocks someone had collected. She removed it, thinking Lourenço may have been the collector.

The second chest was lighter, easier to move, and when she opened it Adrienne saw why. It held a dented silver tea set and candlesticks that were scratched and much tarnished. But mostly it was filled with bundles of paper and several what she took to be ledgers. It had been a long day and she was tired, so thought she would come back later to examine them more carefully, but she riffled through a stack to try to get a sense of what they might be. Her hand landed on something hard at the bottom of the trunk. She pulled it out. An album. Beneath it a sheaf of papers tied with string.

She was about to open the album when Lourenço came back up the stairs. "Look," she said. "Another album."

He sat beside her and they opened it to find the expected photographs but also loose sheets in the back. They put them aside and turned the album pages to find his father, people from the village Lourenço recognized, and others he could not identify. He was naming a few who might be familiar to Adrienne as their children, now adults, still lived in Veredas. He stopped and Adrienne could see one photograph had grabbed his attention.

"What is it?" she asked.

"This photograph. My *pai* and Silvio and Padre Immanuel. He was the priest at the church then. The one my father argued with."

Adrienne looked and saw a stern-faced man standing stiffly between the two young men. His expression was serious, almost grim.

"I remember him, although I was very young when he left. Made an impression on me, I guess."

"I can see why. He seems… *duro,* harsh… forbidding."

Lourenço chuckled and said, "Exactly. Not someone you'd want to make confession to."

They continued their perusal and finding nothing more of particular interest turned to the papers tied with string and those that had fallen from the album.

"It's too dark here to read. Let's finish and take them downstairs. I can look at them later." Lourenço helped Adrienne to her feet and shoved the trunk back into place. She described what the other chests held and showed him the box with shells and rocks. She had been right, he recognized it from boyhood vacations to the shore.

"Maybe I'll give it to Ana for the grandchildren. They might enjoy playing with these."

After dinner, Lourenço went through the papers, opening one, reading it, and setting it aside. Adrienne glanced over to see him shake his head over the stack of handwritten notes that had been in the album.

"The ones tied with string are letters written by my father requesting information and documents he received in return. The others are his handwritten notes. He saved information on every government office he contacted, everyone he wrote to, everything he did to try to find my uncle. There is a lot here. I think I'm too tired to read it all now. But tomorrow I will lay them out and try to make some sense of it."

As they readied for bed, Adrienne asked, "Why do you think this album was in the trunk? Not with the others in the library?"

"I don't know. As I said, my father would disappear into the attic and close the door. Maybe he was re-reading the letters. Maybe he hid it there so my mother would not worry about him, worry that he was obsessed about this. About his inability to find the answers to his questions."

The next morning, she awoke to find Lourenço already up, in the dining room with his coffee, the papers strewn across the table.

"I don't know if I can be of much help. My Portuguese probably isn't good enough to understand the details you might want."

"But yes, you can. There is a date on all the letters and documents. If we put them in order, I can get a better idea of where they fit with my father's notes. Many are dated as well. It might help. Maybe not, but it's a starting point."

When she had poured her coffee and retrieved a pastry from the plate Lourenço had set out, Adrienne started in. He had returned from the library with a new pad of paper to make his own notes and observations. They went about their tasks quietly, with only the occasional interruption of Lourenço's "Hmmm" or "*Ai, eu entendo,* oh, I understand".

Adrienne finished laying out the papers and went to dress as she had arranged to meet Leonor. She hugged him as she left, promising to be back for lunch, and walked down the road.

Sitting at the kitchen table while Leonor made coffee, Adrienne rested her chin in her palms and sighed.

Leonor turned, "*O que?* Something bothering you?"

Adrienne was not sure how much she should share but decided to take the risk and asked, "Do you know about the argument Lourenço's father had with Padre Immanuel?"

"*Não,* not really," said Leonor. "Only what I remember from my mother and father talking about it. I was young." She poured the coffee and sat at the table, removing her glasses and looking off in the distance for a minute.

"Padre Immanuel was not well-liked in Veredas. He had replaced a much-loved priest, Padre Baltasar, who had retired. I would guess people may not have welcomed him as they should have. Started things off on the wrong foot. But then again, he was not a sympathetic man. I remember a number of conversations about him, mostly complaints."

"I saw a photograph of him. He looked so severe."

"*Sim.* He was harsh with his penances." Leonor frowned, then went on, "In any case, there was talk about Lourenço's father, Senhor Madeira, and Padre Immanuel. Something about Silvio, his brother, who had left the village. Went to fight in the Spanish Civil War against the Nationalists. Everyone knew Senhor Madeira had looked for him for years, with no luck. It was complicated by the fact his father, Lourenço's grandfather, did not support this search. Had had a falling out with Silvio about the war. Everyone knew that, too, although no one talked much about it, at least not openly. I heard some saying the grandfather supported the conservative Nationalists. There was also concern about Salazar's increasing authoritarian regime and whether it would bring trouble to the family. Either could have been at the heart of the disagreement between father and son."

"It's such a tangle," sighed Adrienne.

"As I said, I was young and didn't understand what it all meant. Except that Senhor Madeira stopped going to church and even I knew it was an extreme thing to do. In this town where everyone went to church."

When Adrienne returned home, she saw Lourenço, despite the cold, sitting on the front terrace bundled in a heavy jacket. He rose when he saw her on the road and came to greet her. "Is it too cold to walk further? I think I could use the exercise."

He didn't speak as they continued up the hill. Adrienne sensed he needed to take his time before sharing what was on his mind. After some minutes he took her hand and began to talk in a soft voice.

"It weighs heavy on me that I didn't know how hard my father tried to find Silvio. How frustrated he was. How it saddened him his brother was lost. How much he had missed him. Since *Papai* didn't talk about it, I never really understood how close they were. But they were twins, so of course, they must have been. And you can see it in the notes he made. There are references to the many outings they took, places they went in the mountains to the east, people they met. I think *Papai* hoped tracing them might lead to some clue, some idea about where my uncle had gone. Where he ended up. The furthest he got was an exchange with a man the two of them had met on the border between Portugal and Spain. He wrote that Silvio had spent the night with his family on his way to Spain. Nothing of substance turned up after that."

Lourenço stopped, his expression pained. He gave her a sad smile and gestured they should turn back. When they got home, he took her into the dining room to see the orderly piles of documents laid out on the table. As he walked around it, he recited the steps his father had taken in his search, with the piles growing smaller and smaller over time, petering out with a final note written in large letters, *"Não consigo pensar em mais nada para fazer. Ficar a ver navios."*

"I understand the first sentence—I can think of nothing more to do. But what is the second? Left watching ships?"

"It means to be left with nothing." Lourenço stared at the paper, tears finally spilling over. "I know he didn't mean it in the way I am feeling it. But I can't keep the thought from my mind, that my mother and I meant nothing to him." He choked out the last few words.

Adrienne took him in her arms, holding him close. She whispered softly, reassuring him he was right—his father had not meant there was nothing left in his life. She led him into the living room to his favorite chair and sat on the floor beside him, resting her head on his knees.

Silent tears rolled down his cheeks as he took deep breaths, trying to regain control. In time, the breathing quieted. "My mother always said we needed to be compassionate. That we may not understand, but we had to try to forgive my father and be sympathetic with his struggles."

Then Lourenço lifted his shoulder in a half shrug, "One mystery was solved with my search though. There is a note mentioning Padre Immanuel. It says *Papai* asked him to use his contacts in the church to find Silvio. Padre Immanuel refused, saying it was not the church's business. That the church must not be involved in politics in any way. Searching for Silvio could be seen as going against the church and against Salazar. No wonder they argued."

"Actually," said Adrienne, "I asked Leonor if she knew anything about the argument. She told me some time ago her mother and your mother were friends. I thought she might have heard something." Adrienne went on to share what Leonor had told her, ending with, "I hope it was alright. I thought there might be something to help us figure things out."

"*Claro.* Of course. It is long in the past now. I remember my mother trying to explain why my grandfather had fought with Silvio, had not supported his desire to fight in the Spanish Civil War. How they had argued about which side was in the right. And how he worried Silvio's actions would put the family in jeopardy. Salazar's police force was arresting dissidents. Anyone who was speaking out. It must have put my father in great conflict."

Clearing the papers from the table, the two were lost in their own thoughts. Adrienne pondering the idea she had been wrong—Lourenço's early cheerless demeanor had hidden a deep sadness. Not only his loss of Jacolin. It went further back than that. To the sorrow and remorse he felt about his father.

Over dinner, Adrienne asked whether there was anything further he could do to follow up on his father's efforts. "There are a number of books in the library about the Spanish Civil War. Maybe there is something that would help. They're pretty dated, though. Nothing more recent than the 1960s."

"Probably collected by my father. Trying to learn something that would take his search further," Lourenço sighed.

"Records from that period might be more available now. It seems likely someone, university professors or history students, or maybe family members, have investigated the Civil War more thoroughly."

Lourenço looked up, a new light in his eyes. "I hadn't thought of it, but of course. The *Universidade Nova de Lisboa* could be a place to start."

A few telephone calls the next day revealed several research papers about identifying combatant and civilian casualties of the war. Both the *Universidad Complutense de Madrid* and the *Universidad de Barcelona* had some in their collections. There were also books and other references regarding the International Brigades, about the volunteers who joined the fight against the Nationalists. Lourenço had a list of names to write to for further information and had already asked the university in Lisbon if copies of some of the books could be mailed to him.

Chapter 23: *The Call*

Within the month Lourenço was hard at work trying to figure out how he might track Silvio's path during the war. He had also enlisted Fernao to search the internet for more information.

"He says there likely will be something I can use but doubts it will provide everything I need to find Silvio," said Lourenço. "He reminded me the internet is still new. Growing, but limited at this point. He thinks I probably will need to go to Barcelona or Madrid to get the details I want. But he should be able to identify which university has the most complete records and whether there are other resources available."

The phone rang and Lourenço got up to answer it and beckoned for Adrienne. "It's Andy."

She was smiling as she took the phone and greeted him, but her face fell as she listened. She covered the mouthpiece and whispered, "It's my mother. She's had a stroke."

She was quiet as Andy talked, her eyes on Lourenço, then saying, "Yes, of course I'll come. I'll let you know as soon as I make the arrangements."

"She is responding, talking a little," said Andy, "but they don't know yet how much damage the stroke caused. She's asking for you. Oh, wait." Adrienne could hear him talking with someone. Then he was back, "I have to go. The doctor is here and says she seems to be improving. I want to talk with him more."

Lourenço's arms went around her as she called the airline, then he left to get a suitcase from the closet for her clothes. It was late when they made it into bed.

"I know I've told you my mother and I were not close. Especially after my father left. And more so in the last years of my marriage when she always seemed to take Arthur's side." Adrienne nestled into Lourenço's shoulder, her words muffled, "I avoided her because I felt like such a failure… that it was my fault things weren't better for us. I knew it wasn't true, but I still felt that way. Then again, not much about me seemed to please her. I can't help but wonder why she's asking for me."

Lourenço cradled her. "Maybe she regrets how hard she's been on you. Wants to make amends."

Adrienne thought about it a moment. "Maybe, but it would surprise me. She has never been one for deep introspection. Or backtracking. I don't think I've ever heard her say she was wrong." Then reluctantly, "I guess I should keep an open mind though. You might be right."

≈≈≈≈≈≈≈

Despite his wish to drive her to the airport, Adrienne insisted Aveiro was far enough. The morning train would get her to Lisbon in plenty of time to catch the plane. As they parted, Lourenço kissed her gently and held her against his chest.

"I hope your mother is alright. And there is a good reason, I mean, a positive reason why she is calling for you."

Adrienne kept the thought in her heart on the train trip south, but on the plane, she reflected how the last time she had flown west her attention had been solely on what lay ahead in New Jersey and what her life would be like. This time her thoughts were divided—on her mother and her mother's future, but equally, on what she was leaving—Lourenço and a life firmly planted in Portugal.

The shuttle from La Guardia to Camden took more than two hours, dropping her at a downtown hotel where Andy picked her up. On the way to the hospital, he gave her an update on their mother's health.

"She's more alert. Her speech is improving. I can understand almost everything now. Yesterday the doctor says if she continues to improve, she can go to the nursing wing that's connected to her apartment complex."

"Really? That's great to hear."

"Well, she won't like it I imagine. But it is out of my hands. I haven't told her yet. She's regained her usual attitude. Complaining. About the care she is getting, the nurses, the bed, the food. Maybe the fact that she'll be one step closer to home will calm her down. She's still asking for you, by the way, and I let her know you'd be here soon."

"Did she say why?" Adrienne hesitated. "I mean, it surprises me. We haven't been… close for some years. I guess that's the nicest way to say it."

"No, she didn't say. Just that she wanted to see you."

It was with some trepidation Adrienne entered the hospital room. Her mother's eyes were closed, her face peaceful. She drew in a slow breath as she sat next to the bed. Her thoughts went to Lourenço and his hope for a reconciliation of some kind.

Her mother's eyes opened and she found Adrienne's face. Her mouth turned down into a lopsided scowl.

"Well, there you are. Took your time." The words were slurred but clear enough. Adrienne flinched. *So much for atonement*, she thought.

Although it was clear that speaking was not easy, her mother seemed to gain momentum with each sentence.

"You... you were never there for me. Couldn't be bothered. Then up and went to that place. Left it all to Andy. Then he went off and left me, too. Twice, and at Christmas! And now this. Having to be in this place. I'm going to need help. Andy can't do it. He has his work and his kids. You have nothing but a dream." She was out of breath, glaring at Adrienne.

She could feel the guilt rising in her. It came flooding back immediately—the little jabs starting when she became a teenager—she wasn't thin enough, didn't take care of her hair, wasn't choosing the best clothes, didn't have the right friends. As she got older her mother continued to berate her for not being smart enough for college or getting a decent job. For not being good enough—a good enough daughter, a good enough wife.

Adrienne shrank back in her chair. The familiar feeling of inadequacy overwhelmed her. She said nothing. And she thought, *yes, just a dream, a dream of a new life.* When her mother turned her face away, she stood and left the room, tears now running down her cheeks. She ducked into the women's room, avoiding Andy who was coming out of the elevator. She thanked god it was empty and locked herself in a stall and wept.

It took her some time to regain her composure, wash her face, and walk back out into the corridor. Of course, she could not hide her distress from Andy, who wrapped his arms around her and began to whisper in her ear. "It's okay, it's okay."

This brought on another wave of tears she tried to hold back. "I just… I can't… I'm sorry… " She leaned against him and choked out, "It took me back to when I was a kid. And later. I was never good enough. Could never satisfy her. Always felt ashamed that I couldn't measure up." She took a breath and sighed, "I thought I had put it behind me. I guess not."

Andy took Adrienne's arm and led her into an empty adjacent hallway. "You have nothing to be ashamed of." He looked directly into her eyes, his voice firm. "Our mother has been unhappy most of her life. She took it out on you. Why you and not me, I don't know. I didn't do anything special. I wasn't without my faults. I often wondered if she was projecting something on you, something she felt about herself and why Dad left us."

His words calmed her. A little. She wasn't convinced, wasn't alright, but she stopped crying. They stood in silence for a minute, then she stepped back and nodded her head toward their mother's room. "You go ahead."

Adrienne sat in the waiting room while Andy went in to visit their mother. She was not about to subject herself to more haranguing. And she needed to consider what Andy had said. Their mother being so unhappy. With so much abuse heaped on her, she had not thought about its origins. One more thing to feel guilty about.

In the car on the way to Andy's house, she tried to explore this further. Get some clue, some insight into her mother's behavior.

"We never talked about it," Adrienne said. "Well, she wouldn't. Refused to say why Dad left or where he went. And never talked about the divorce, except that she had made sure he would never be a part of our lives again. So, it was like he fell off the face of the earth. I wonder if he tried to see us."

"I wondered, too. A few times I thought I saw him. Driving by the school or on a street by the house."

"You never told me."

"I wasn't sure. And I was scared to bring it up. I don't know why." He glanced over at her, "I tried to find him… a couple of years ago. I was just learning about the internet and what it could do. There was nothing. There probably is more now. I haven't thought to look again."

Adrienne went to bed thinking about it. Looking for the starting point. Yes, maybe shortly after her father had left. The reproaches weren't daily, weren't unrelenting. Could she remember if certain things set them off? Trigger points? She wrestled with her memories trying to put her finger on anything specific. Finally, it came to her. The beginning of every month. Her job had been to bring in the mail and without knowing why, she began to worry at the sight of the monthly bank statement. She had chalked it up to concern about not having enough money, something her mother continually harped on. Would there have been a deposit she saw each month? Alimony? Child support? Certainly, if she had prevented their father from seeing them, her mother would have won a decent settlement.

In the morning they sat at the breakfast table, both exhausted from tossing and turning and the worry. Adrienne looked up from her coffee and asked Andy if he knew anything about the divorce settlement, about money coming in each month. He had taken over the bill-paying and checkbook-balancing for his mother a few years ago.

"Not that I remember. By the time I took over it was only Social Security. But she did have, and still does, a sizable amount in her savings account. I wondered about it but didn't ask. You know, she was so touchy about money. Always talking about not having enough and needing to save. I never went back to her old statements to see where it came from."

"Does she still have the old statements? We could look to see if money had been coming in from somewhere else."

"Only the last five years, from when I took over the bill-paying. I got rid of the older ones, took them to my accountant for shredding. But she's used the same bank forever. We probably can request old statements."

As they drove to the hospital later, Adrienne shared the other things that had kept her awake most of the night. How maybe her life in Portugal was just a pipe dream. How maybe she needed to be here to help. And most of all, how little she had thought about her mother's unhappiness.

"I know I was hurt by Mom's criticisms and lecturing, but I can't help feeling guilty for not seeing her pain."

Andy put up a hand to stop her. "No more guilt. I know it's probably useless to say it, but you have to give yourself a break. She was plain mean to you. And you were only a teenager. How could you be expected to figure out why? And… " he pulled the car over so he could look directly at her and took both her hands in his. "I don't want to hear any of this bullshit about you not having a life in Portugal. You do have a life there and you deserve it. You've come into your own there. And Mom will get all the care she needs. She'll have help. It won't all fall to me."

Adrienne burst into tears. "I seem to be doing this a lot," she choked out. It took a minute, but finally, she squeezed his hands, "Thank you. I really do know I have a life in Veredas, a life with Lourenço. But hearing you say it out loud helps me believe it."

"You go first," Adrienne said when they exited the hospital elevator. "I need to prepare myself." Andy shrugged and responded with, "If you say so. But maybe it will be easier if we go in together."

"No, I need to figure out how to be with her. And you shouldn't have to listen to more of her complaints and ranting at me."

While she waited, Adrienne thought about her mother and the life she had led after her father left. Out of nowhere, what Lourenço had said about compassion came to her—what his mother had said about not necessarily being able to understand someone or help them, but that should not keep you from being sympathetic to what they were experiencing.

When Andy came out, he jerked his head in the direction of their mother's room and said, "Maybe she tired herself out complaining. She seemed to run out of steam at the end."

Adrienne took a deep breath, walked in, and sat by the bed. Her mother started right in, shaking her head and looking to the ceiling. She was repeating the complaints Andy had shared about the room, the food, the scratchy hospital gown. On how uncomfortable she was, and no one seemed to care. But as Andy said, eventually she slowed down. Adrienne reached out and took her hand, softly stroking it and saying, "I'm so sorry, Mom. I wish I could make it better."

"Well, I… " her mother sputtered, then stopped and looked into Adrienne's face. Tears welled in her eyes. "I just want to go home."

Adrienne nodded, and said, "You will. Andy talked with the doctor. You're getting better and the place where you live has a unit where there are nurses and physical therapists. You'll have to stay there for a while to get stronger, but you'll be out of the hospital and almost home."

She steeled herself for a tirade about the nursing wing and how awful it would probably be. But no, her mother simply looked at her and said, "Okay." She sat quietly until her mother dropped off, murmuring a bit when Adrienne tucked her hand under the covers and left. She saw Andy in the waiting room and went quickly to him, hugging him, stepping back, and telling him what had transpired.

"I can't believe it," she said. "It was like a switch just turned off. And when I told her about the nursing unit, she said okay, then fell asleep."

Before they left, they spoke with the doctor who let them know arrangements were being made at the assisted living facility. A room in the nursing unit would be available for their mother in a couple of days.

Chapter 24: *Uncovering*

They got take-out for an early dinner, feeling any interaction with waiters at a restaurant was too much to cope with. As Adrienne put the food in the oven to keep warm, Andy was on the phone with the bank.

"You got me curious," he said as he hung up. "Mom's bank can order the statements. It'll take a couple of days, but they're mailing them."

"I didn't set a date for my return to Portugal, not knowing what was going to happen. I can stay. I want to wait until Mom's out of the hospital anyway. Now I want to see if there is anything in the bank statements. But, before we eat, can I call Lourenço? I'd like to tell him what's going on."

When she went into the living room to make her call, Andy pulled out his laptop, a new Compaq he had purchased recently. He typed in a command to search the internet for his father's name. It had been almost three years since he had last looked. Maybe there was something now.

Adrienne came back into the kitchen glowing from her conversation with Lourenço, only to see Andy staring at the computer, a look on his face she couldn't quite interpret. "What is it?"

He turned the computer toward her as she sat at the table. The screen showed an obituary. Her father's name at the top. It read:

Dean Andrew Banks

Born in Philadelphia, Pennsylvania on November 6, 1922 to Howard and Margaret Banks. Died on February 2, 1994 in Carlisle, Pennsylvania of a heart attack. Dean was a much-respected financial analyst and a valued member of the Carlisle Chamber of Commerce and the YMCA where he had been a volunteer coach for many years. He cared deeply about and will be missed by his family, his golfing buddies, and the community of longtime friends at the United Methodist Church.

Dean is survived by his wife Angela, son Christian and his wife Barbara, their two sons, and a daughter and son from a previous marriage, Adrienne Banks Martin of New Brunswick, NJ and Andrew Banks of Camden, NJ and his daughter and son.

Services will be held at the United Methodist Church on Saturday, February 19, at 2:00 pm. In lieu of flowers, please consider a donation to the American Heart Association or a YMCA in your community.

"He knew about us." Adrienne raised a trembling hand to her mouth. "Where we lived. That I had gotten married. That you had Kathyrn and Jake."

"Not only that," said Andy. "His wife knew as well. She would have been the one to put the obituary in the paper."

They were silent, rereading, looking at each other and back to the screen. Numbly, Adrienne dished out their dinner. Andy closed the laptop and set the table.

"And he was close by. I mean, Carlisle isn't far. On the other side of Harrisburg, a couple of hours away." Andy was shaking his head. "I wonder if Mom knew."

"If she cut him out of her life, out of our lives, how would she know?"

"I don't know." Andy stared glumly at his plate. They picked at their food, and with a hug, went to bed to try to catch up on their sleep.

Andy seemed to have shaken off much of his gloom by morning, coming into the kitchen where Adrienne was making breakfast. "I woke up thinking how sad it was we missed out having our dad with us. Then I remembered the words in the obituary about his family and how he cared for them deeply. That included us. Even though he hadn't seen us for years and years. Well, maybe he saw us, but he didn't get to talk with us, get to know us. So, sad for him, too. But he had a life that somehow included us. Where we were still family. I don't know... it made me feel better."

Adrienne wasn't sure how she felt. Sad, certainly, but in a distant way. A part of her father's family? She wasn't sure about that either. It, too, seemed far away. She would continue to ponder that detached feeling all day, wondering why she didn't feel more connected. Perhaps her ties in the States were loosening as those in Veredas were getting stronger.

Two days later Adrienne and Andy accompanied their mother's ambulance from the hospital to the care facility. As they helped get her into her room, they noticed the slower, more slurred speech and a weariness about her movements as the staff settled her in bed.

"It's been a tiring day, Mom," Andy said. "You probably should get some rest. Is there anything you need from your apartment?"

"Oh, yes. Please." She pointed to her hospital gown. "Would you go get my nice nightgown? And the robe from my closet? I'd like some of my things around me."

As Andy went to fetch the requested items, Adrienne sat alongside her mother, stroking her arm, and watching her face soften as she drifted into sleep.

≈≈≈≈≈≈≈

They returned the following morning to find their mother reverting to her usual, more querulous self. Complaints that this was not the pink nightgown she had wanted, and would Andy bring more than one so she could change them. "And slippers, too."

Andy and Adrienne exchanged smiles as he left. She interrupted the continued mutterings to tell her mother Kathryn and Jake would be stopping by in the afternoon to say hello. She went on with unimportant small talk Andy had shared about his children—Kathryn's enjoyment of art school and how well Jake seemed to be doing in his last year of high school. She caught herself and stopped talking abruptly before revealing Jake's happiness at being accepted to the university in Lisbon. She did not want to start down a track that could only end up with her mother's resentment about more people leaving her.

Andy saved the bell by coming in with an armload of clothes he hung in the closet and put into the dresser drawers. "Nightgowns, robes, a bed jacket, slippers, socks, underwear, and some stretchy pants and shirts that might work when you start physical therapy. And here's the nice throw from the couch." Their mother actually smiled.

Adrienne was able to catch up with Kathryn and Jake over dinner that evening, as well as enjoy their reminiscences about the trip to Portugal. They knew of her move to Lourenço's, but she brought them up to date on Ana and Fernao and their children and described the joyous Christmas they had shared. She also told them of Lourenço's efforts to find information about his uncle and having leads to new sources in Spain. Jake was particularly enthusiastic.

"I'm going to be at the *Universidade de Lisboa* and will have access to the library. Maybe I can help. Unless he finds everything he needs before I get there. I'm planning to come over at the end of June to look for a place to stay and start to work on my Portuguese. I've gotten some taped lessons from the library here in Camden, but that will only take me so far."

"I don't know if Lourenço knows anyone in Lisbon who could help with an apartment, but I'll ask him. And I'll tell you from my own experience, if you can find a Portuguese tutor, it makes a big difference. I'd be happy to pay for it. Here and in Lisbon. As a birthday gift… it's coming up soon, right?"

Despite his protestations, Adrienne made sure to write him a decent-sized check before he left. One for Kathryn, too, to be fair, but also to help with new expenses as she was planning a move to Philadelphia in a few months to start a summer internship. Something she had pursued after the conversation she had had with Ana.

Clean-up done, Adrienne and Andy collapsed in the living room for a nightcap before bed, tired from the emotional day. "Your kids are great, Andy. I'm so excited to see how determined they are about going after what they want. Like Kathryn and this internship at the art gallery. It sounds perfect."

"Thanks for your support, the checks I mean. I make plenty but am careful about handing it out to them. So, I know the money will be appreciated."

"I'm happy to help. What with moving in with Lourenço and the money Arthur left me, I'm doing fine. Better than fine, actually. I meant to say something earlier but forgot in all the comings and goings. If I can do something for Mom, money-wise, I hope you'll tell me. I know you said she has a reasonable savings account, but maybe being in this new unit while still keeping her apartment is going to be expensive."

"I checked yesterday. Medicare will cover the nursing unit for a month and most of the cost of the physical therapy And I don't know if she'll need to stay so long. The doctor seemed pretty optimistic about her recovery."

"Well, if there's anything, please let me know."

The arrival of her mother's bank statements dispelled any qualms Adrienne had about not having contributed anything in the past. "$188,712 in her savings? And that's in addition to what you have invested for her? How much was that? Another couple hundred thousand? I didn't realize there was so much."

"Yeah, and it's all still there. More now with the interest. She hasn't spent a dime of it since she bought the condominium. I keep telling her the money in savings will do her more good if we move it into the investment fund, but she's old school. I think she'd keep it under her mattress if I let her."

When they went back through each year, they quickly found what they were searching for. A $150,000 deposit into savings in April 1994, six years ago. "A life insurance policy?" asked Adrienne.

"It's likely. He was a financial analyst. And look! Before that, there was a monthly deposit into her checking account of $200."

"He was paying alimony all these years? That's... I don't know. Outrageous."

"The rules may have been different when they divorced. It wouldn't be so long now. Or maybe he simply continued to pay." Andy laughed, "I don't feel so bad about paying CiCi for the last two years. With just one more to go unless she marries the boyfriend."

They sat and stared at the papers in front of them. Adrienne said, "There must have been child support, too. At least until we were out of the house."

"I didn't think to ask for bank statements back so far. It's no wonder Mom had enough. Not just to keep the house while we were growing up, but to buy her condo outright. As well as have so much left to invest and put into savings."

"Do you know what she intends to do with it? When she goes, I mean. You're the executor, aren't you?"

"Yes. I have a copy of her will. It's pretty simple, saying the estate should be divided between the four of us. You, me, Kathryn and Jake."

"Oh. I… I didn't know. I was curious. I'm so glad Kathryn and Jake are named. It will provide a good cushion for both of them. As you said, Mom always made such a point about not having money. It made me feel like I had to be careful all the time." Adrienne sighed. "And I guess I took that into my marriage with Arthur. He was pretty tight with money, too. One more thing I had to tiptoe around."

"It's funny.," said Andy. "Here we are in our 50s and just now talking about things like this."

"I know. It's wonderful. I feel like the weight I've carried around all these years is falling away. It started with Lourenço. I know I told you how gruff and unapproachable he was when I first met him. That changed. He started opening up. A little at a time. I think he was letting go of things, burdens he had been carrying."

Adrienne tilted her head and smiled. "It gave me permission to as well. I can't say I'm free of them. Nor is he. Not of everything. And it's rubbed off on me. I feel more content with myself."

Andy nudged her shoulder. "Except for the small meltdown at the hospital, I can see it, too. You're allowed, you know."

Chapter 25: *Back Again*

With one last visit to her mother two days later, Adrienne and Andy had a final lunch out before her shuttle left for LaGuardia. The night flight to Lisbon would be grueling, but she hoped she would be able to sleep at least part of the way.

As they waited for the bus to load, she hugged him for about the tenth time and said, "I think it's great you're encouraging Jake to go to Lisbon by himself instead of you going along to help him with the apartment hunt. But I hope you'll come visit soon."

"We'll see. I'm hoping Fernao and I can put together a plan for a joint venture. He's got some good ideas about this network his company is a part of. It would be easier, and more fun, to work on them in person. The internet and email are fine, but it's not the same."

"Well, you're always welcome in Veredas. And I'm sure it's true for Ana and Fernao in Porto, too. If not sooner, maybe Christmas? With Kathryn?"

"Sooner than that if I can."

As she started on her marathon journey, Adrienne looked out the shuttle window and let herself dream of a family reunion. The sweet images stayed with her as she drank a glass of wine on the plane and settled in for the long trip.

To her surprise, she saw a familiar face outside customs when she arrived in Lisbon. "What are you doing here?" she said as she approached him.

Without a word, Lourenço took her in his arms and gave her a long hungry kiss. She flung her arms around him and returned it, lips hard against his. Adrienne giggled as she drew back and became aware of other travelers eyeing them with charmed smiles.

Always so calm, he was practically bouncing on his toes alongside her. "I missed you. Couldn't wait for the train. I was… " he searched for the words and said, "*Comer o pão que o diabo amassou.*"

"Eat the bread the devil prepared?" asked Adrienne. "I don't know what that means."

"It means to suffer. To suffer too much."

She laughed, "Your suffering is over. I am home." She took his arm and did not let it go until they reached the car and he loaded her suitcase into the trunk.

On the drive north, she told him of the last days of her visit, about her mother's improvement, and the possibility of a visit from Andy in the fall. He let her know he had contacted an acquaintance at the university in Lisbon who promised help with Jake's apartment hunt and began to describe the progress he and Fernao had made searching for Silvio—tracing him to Albacete, the headquarters for International Brigade volunteers fighting the Nationalists in Spain, and from there to a battalion heading to the rugged northeastern part of the country.

About to go on with more details about what they uncovered, Lourenço looked over and saw Adrienne had nodded off, her head resting on the car window. He stopped talking, concentrating on the highway and the last hour of the drive.

She awakened at the sharp turn the road took near Veredas and was reminded of her first visit, the expansive view to the distant Atlantic, and how the village nestled into the hills. It was too foggy to see the coastline today, but the old stone buildings with their wrought-iron ringed balconies and the familiar storefronts, the small plaza, and Nicholau's restaurant warmed her heart.

≈≈≈≈≈≈≈

Within a day Adrienne recovered from the jetlag and walked into the village. A stop at Leonor's turned into a lengthy coffee klatch to tell her of the trip to New Jersey, her mother's recovery, and an update on Andy and his children.

Leonor smiled at her friend. "I can see something in you. An easiness. No, a peace I have not seen before. Your return this time is different."

"Yes, I thought I was coming home last time. I hoped so but wasn't sure. Now, *sim. Tenho certeza.* I am sure. Home."

Leonor had news of her own. "Carolina has joined me in the company. I mean, officially, not working for me but as a partner. She is full of ideas. Ready to expand."

"And you thought this would be just a retirement hobby!"

They talked of other goings-on in the village. The new pharmacist's wife opening the health clinic. A second guesthouse coming soon, based on the success of Benita's. Marissa and Marcos expecting a baby.

Dinner at Pap'açorda later in the week revealed another surprise. Rehe peeked out from the kitchen door and waved.

"He's been asking to watch me in the kitchen for a while," said Nicholau. "I thought, why not? Two nights a week for now, but if things go well, he can add more days when he is finished with school. Business has been picking up. I'm getting older and could use an assistant. Marissa isn't interested in becoming a chef. We'll see if Rehe likes it once he understands how much work it is."

Lourenço and Adrienne caught up on the other gossip and teased Marissa about her coming event. She glowed as she reported Adao was promoting Marcos at the bakery.

They walked through the garden in the morning, talking of the spring weather and admiring the early blossoms and bulbs sprouting. "We should go to the shore," said Lourenço. "The beginning of April is my favorite time of year there. It is warming up, but still cool enough to keep many of the tourists away."

And they did just that a few weeks later…

Adrienne sat facing the sea, leaning back in her beach chair, drawing a hand through the sand while Lourenço went back to the car for the picnic basket. She thought of her first stay on the coast two years ago—that grim bus tour and her escape to Veredas. So much had happened since then. So much unexpected joy. And she thought, with no doubts in the back of her mind, *I never held out the hope that my life would have such a happy ending.*

Acknowledgements

Great thanks go to my first readers Hal Burton, Wendy Hagen Bauer and Shawna Bliss. Their enthusiasm for the story made me believe this book should go forward. Their comments, suggestions and corrections helped make it happen. And again, to Wendy and Andrea Wiley, their help with the Portuguese was invaluable.

My love and thanks, as well, to Sally Marts for the stellar work on the book cover and the always welcome artist-eye.

I also want to acknowledge the Hood Canal Writer's Group—a home, a safe space for sharing, feedback and support. Thank you to all its members.

To Judith Clegg, Lynn Davison, and Joan Raymond for unending encouragement. And to other friends and my family for putting up with my distracted days at the computer.

More by the Author

Crossing Time in Pine Creek

Here's what readers have said about the book...

I climbed into this book... connecting with the characters who were real people, honestly caring for each other, and trying to get through hard times. The main character Jason's growth as he pursues Civil War historical research and experiences support and guidance from friends and the local librarian expands the story as it explores fascinating and unexpected historical details and connections. I highly recommend this read!!

I enjoyed every moment of this novel and became so fond of the characters I didn't want it to end. It is a warm and wonderful story that will appeal to all age groups, male and female. All libraries, including schools and churches, should have a copy, or two!

What a great read! Seriously, once I started it, I was always unhappy whenever I had to put it down. Working on the mystery of it all was fascinating, especially the inter-generational sleuthing. All in all, I can honestly declare that I enjoyed reading the book. Not as in "I enjoyed reading it because my friend Dawn wrote it", although that was special, too, but straight up "I enjoyed reading it".

This book is a gentle escape to a comfortable place through the turning of a phrase, or a path through a silvan wood. It also shows to all, especially the young, the importance of connecting and collaborating with people with similar interests. The gentle plot allows one to surrender to the simplicity of real life, which if pursued with some grit and a good heart, can bring good fortune.